The Great Gatsby Unbound

F. SCOTT FITZGERALD
AND
KARENA ROSE

piatkus

PIATKUS

First published in Great Britain in 2013 by Piatkus

Copyright © 2013 Karena Rose

A CIP catalogue record for this book
is available from the British Library.

ISBN 978-0-349-40046-4

Typeset in Garamond by M Rules
Printed and bound in Great Britain by
Clays Ltd, St Ives, plc

Papers used by Piatkus are from well-managed forests
and other responsible sources.

MIX
Paper from
responsible sources
FSC® C104740

Piatkus
An imprint of
Little, Brown Book Group
100 Victoria Embankment
London EC4Y 0DY

An Hachette UK Company
www.hachette.co.uk

www.piatkus.co.uk

To Boo, Delilah and Jessie

Prologue

In my younger and more vulnerable years my father gave me some advice that I've been turning over in my mind ever since.

'Whenever you feel like criticising anyone,' he told me, 'just remember that all the people in this world haven't had the advantages that you've had.'

He didn't say any more, but we've always been unusually communicative in a reserved way, and I understood that he meant a great deal more than that. In consequence, I'm inclined to reserve all judgements, a habit that has opened up many curious natures to me and also made me the victim of not a few veteran bores. The abnormal mind is quick to detect and attach itself to this quality when it appears in a normal person, and so it came about that in college I was unjustly accused of being a politician, because

I was privy to the secret griefs of wild, unknown men. Most of the confidences were unsought – frequently I have feigned sleep, preoccupation, or a hostile levity when I realised by some unmistakable sign that an intimate revelation was quivering on the horizon; for the intimate revelations of young men, or at least the terms in which they express them, are usually plagiaristic and marred by obvious suppressions. Reserving judgements is a matter of infinite hope. I am still a little afraid of missing something if I forget that, as my father snobbishly suggested, and I snobbishly repeat, a sense of the fundamental decencies is parcelled out unequally at birth.

And, after boasting this way of my tolerance, I come to the admission that it has a limit. Conduct may be founded on the hard rock or the wet marshes, but after a certain point I don't care what it's founded on. When I came back from the East last autumn I felt that I wanted the world to be in uniform and at a sort of moral attention for ever; I wanted no more riotous excursions with privileged glimpses into the human heart. Only Gatsby, the man who gives his name to this book, was exempt from my reaction – Gatsby, who represented everything for which I have an unaffected scorn. If personality is an unbroken series of successful gestures, then there was something gorgeous about him, some heightened sensitivity to the promises of life, as if he were related to one of those intricate machines that register earthquakes ten thousand miles away. This responsiveness had nothing to do with that flabby impressionability which is dignified under the name of the 'creative temperament' – it was an extraordinary gift for hope, a romantic readiness such as I have never found in any other person and which it is not likely I shall ever find again. No – Gatsby turned out all right at the end; it is what preyed on Gatsby, what foul dust floated in the wake of his dreams that temporarily closed out my interest in the abortive sorrows and short-winded elations of men.

Chapter One

My family have been prominent, frigid people for three generations. The Carraways are something of a cold clan, a virtuous, well-to-do lot who muffle lust with hard, shiny money. But the actual founder of my line, I have learnt from scandalised whispers and rumours, was far more debauched than my ancestors would like to admit. He was my grandfather's brother, and he came here in '51, sent a substitute to the Civil War, and started the wholesale hardware business that my father carries on today. Having secured a reasonable nest egg, he frittered the rest on gambling and whores. Despite being no beauty, I have heard he was charismatic and more than one good lady's reputation was sullied by his dirty paws. Sadly I never saw this great-uncle, but I'm supposed to look like him – with special reference to the rather hard-boiled painting that hangs in my father's office. I just wish our accomplishments matched in other ways.

I graduated from New Haven in 1915 a virgin, which is more of an achievement than it sounds. Any attempt made in that area was obstructed by my own quiet nature, though I certainly wished to be relieved of such a burden. However, I had little time to dwell on this before participating in that delayed Teutonic migration known as the Great War. My pent-up desires served me well as unquenchable stores of aggression there and I enjoyed the counter-raid so thoroughly that I came back restless.

Instead of being the warm centre of the world it had been, the Middle West now seemed like the ragged edge of the universe – so I decided to go East and learn the bond business. Everybody I knew was in the bond business, so I supposed it could support one more single man. I had heard that it was a profession that attracted women and my peers from New Haven were prime examples of this, if their erotic, carnal tales were to be believed. My aunts and uncles talked over my decision as if they were choosing a prep school for me, and finally said, 'Why – ye – es,' with very grave, hesitant faces. Then father agreed to finance me for a year, and after various delays I came East, permanently, I thought, in the spring of '22.

It was a warm season and the first practical thing was to find rooms in the city, but I had just left a country of wide lawns and friendly trees, so when a young man at the office suggested that we take a house together in a commuting town, it sounded like a great idea. I knew him to be a rake and I had hoped that some of his debonair attraction might rub off on me. We found a house, a weather-beaten cardboard bungalow at eighty a month, but at the last minute the firm ordered him to Washington, and instead I went out to the country alone. I had a dog – at least I had him for a few days until he ran away – and an old Dodge and a Finnish woman, who made my bed and cooked breakfast and muttered Finnish wisdom to herself over the electric stove.

It was lonely for a day or so until one morning some man, more recently arrived than I, stopped me on the road.

'How do you get to West Egg village?' he asked helplessly.

I told him. And as I walked on I was lonely no longer. I was a guide, a pathfinder, an original settler. He had casually conferred on me the freedom of the neighbourhood. And so with the sunshine and the great bursts of leaves growing on the trees, just as things grow in fast movies, I had that familiar conviction that life was beginning over again with the summer.

It was a matter of chance that I should have rented a house in one of the strangest communities in North America. It was on that slender riotous island which extends itself due east of New York – and where there are, among other natural curiosities, two unusual formations of land. Twenty miles from the city a pair of enormous eggs, identical in contour and separated only by a courtesy bay, jut out into the most domesticated body of salt water in the Western hemisphere, the great wet barnyard of Long Island Sound. They are not perfect ovals – like the egg in the Columbus story, they are both crushed flat at the contact end – their physical resemblance is closer to two pert, heavy breasts.

I lived at West Egg, the – well, the less fashionable of the two, though this is a most superficial tag to express the bizarre and not a little sinister contrast between them. My house was at the very tip of the egg, only fifty yards from the Sound, and squeezed between two huge places that rented for twelve or fifteen thousand a season. The one on my right was a colossal affair by any standard – it was a factual imitation of some hotel de ville in Normandy, with a tower on one side, spanking new under a thin beard of raw ivy, and a marble swimming pool, and more than forty acres of lawn and garden. It was Gatsby's fantastic mansion.

Or, rather, as I didn't know Mr Gatsby at the time, it was a mansion inhabited by a gentleman of that name. My own house was an eyesore, but it was a small eyesore, and it had been overlooked, so I had a view of the water, a partial view of my neighbour's lawn, and the consoling proximity of millionaires – all for eighty dollars a month.

Across the courtesy bay the white palaces of fashionable East Egg glittered along the water, and the history of my summer really begins on the evening I drove over there to have dinner with the Buchanans. There my latent desire was finally quenched and my burning thirst for more began. I met a golden, hard girl who changed everything.

Chapter Two

Daisy Buchanan was my second cousin once removed, and I'd known Tom Buchanan in college. Among various physical accomplishments, Tom had been one of the most powerful ends that ever played football at New Haven – a national figure in a way, one of those men who reach such an acute limited excellence at twenty-one that everything afterwards savours of anticlimax. His family were enormously wealthy – even in college his freedom with money was a matter for reproach – but now he'd left Chicago and come East in a fashion that rather took your breath away: for instance, he'd brought down a string of polo ponies from Lake Forest. It was hard to realise that a man in my own generation was wealthy enough to do that.

Why they came East I don't know. They had spent a year in France for no particular reason, and then drifted here and there unrestfully wherever people played polo and were rich together. This was a 'permanent' move, said Daisy over the telephone, but I didn't believe it – I had no sight into Daisy's heart, but I felt that Tom would drift on forever seeking, a little wistfully, for the dramatic turbulence of some irrecoverable football game.

And so it happened that on a warm windy evening I drove over to East Egg to see two old friends whom I scarcely knew at all. Their house was even more elaborate than I expected, a cheerful red-and-white Georgian Colonial mansion, overlooking the bay. The lawn started at the beach and ran towards the front door for a quarter of a mile, jumping over sun-dials and brick walks and burning gardens – finally when it reached the house drifting up the side in bright vines as though from the momentum of its run. The front was broken by a line of French windows, glowing now with reflected gold and wide open to the warm windy afternoon, and Tom Buchanan in riding clothes was standing with his legs apart on the front porch.

He had changed since his New Haven years. Now he was a sturdy straw-haired man of thirty with a rather hard mouth and a supercilious manner. Two shining arrogant eyes had established dominance over his face and gave him the appearance of always leaning aggressively forwards. Not even the effeminate swank of his riding clothes could hide the enormous power of that body – he seemed to fill those glistening boots until he strained the top lacing, and you could see a great pack of muscle shifting when his shoulders moved under his thin coat. It was a body capable of enormous leverage – a cruel body. It was an immense favourite with the girls of whom there had been many. I had always looked on Tom rather jealously in our New Haven days as he touted about blonde, thin things and dragged them to his godlike level. Even his voice, a gruff husky tenor, added to the impression of fractiousness he conveyed. There was a touch of paternal contempt in it, even towards people he liked – and there were men at New Haven who had hated his guts. 'Now, don't think my opinion on these matters is final,' his manner seemed to say, 'just because I'm stronger and more of a man than you are.'

We were in the same senior society at New Haven, and while we were never intimate I always had the impression that he approved of me and wanted me to like him with some harsh, defiant wistfulness of his own. I could see it even as we stood on that sunny porch in front of his vast mansion that afternoon.

'I've got a nice place here,' he said, his eyes flashing about restlessly.

Turning me around by one arm, he moved a broad flat hand along the front vista, including in its sweep a sunken Italian garden, a half-acre of deep, pungent roses, and a snub-nosed motor boat that bumped the tide offshore.

'It belonged to Demaine, the oilman.' He turned me around again, politely and abruptly. 'We'll go inside.'

We walked through a high hallway into a bright rosy-coloured space, fragilely bound into the house by French windows at either end. The windows were ajar and gleaming white against the fresh grass outside that seemed to grow a little way into the house. A breeze blew through the room, blew curtains in at one end and out the other like pale flags, twisting them up towards the frosted wedding-cake of the ceiling, and then rippled over the wine-coloured rug, making a shadow on it as wind does on the sea.

The only completely stationary object in the room was an enormous couch on which two young women were buoyed up as though upon an anchored balloon. They were both in white, and their dresses were rippling and fluttering as if they had just been blown back in after a short flight around the house. I must have stood for a few moments listening to the whip and snap of the curtains and the groan of a picture on the wall. Then there was a boom as Tom Buchanan shut the rear windows and the caught wind died out about the room, and the curtains and the rugs and the two young women ballooned slowly to the floor.

The younger of the two was a stranger to me. She was extended full length at her end of the divan, completely motionless, and with her chin raised a little, as if she were balancing something on it which was quite likely to fall. If she saw me out of the corner of her cat-like eyes then she gave no hint of it – indeed, I was almost surprised into murmuring an apology for having disturbed her by coming in. She had hair so dark that it smouldered and unfashionably large breasts that she did nothing to disguise. They hung lazily beneath her dress, her nipples erect through the fabric. I liked her immediately and I felt my breath go a little shaky.

The other girl was Daisy, Tom's last thin thing, or so I thought. She made an attempt to rise – she leaned slightly forwards with a conscientious expression – then she laughed, an absurd, charming little laugh, and I laughed too and came forwards into the room.

'I'm p-paralysed with happiness.' She laughed again, as if she said something very witty, and held my hand for a moment, looking up into my face, promising that there was no one in the world she so much wanted to see. That was a way she had. She hinted in a murmur that the surname of the other girl was Baker. (I've heard it said that Daisy's murmur was only to make people lean towards her; an irrelevant criticism that made it no less charming.)

At any rate, Miss Baker's cushioned lips fluttered, she nodded at me almost imperceptibly, and then quickly tipped her head back again – the object she was balancing had obviously tottered a little and given her something of a fright. Again a sort of apology arose to my lips. Almost any exhibition of complete self-sufficiency draws a stunned tribute from me.

I looked back at my cousin, who began to ask me questions in her low, thrilling voice. It was the kind of voice that the ear follows up and down, as if each speech is an arrangement of notes that will never be played again. Her face was sad and lovely with bright things in it, bright eyes and a bright passionate mouth, but there was an excitement in her voice that men who had cared for her found difficult to forget: a singing compulsion, a whispered 'Listen,' a promise that she had done gay, exciting things just a while since and that there were gay, exciting things hovering in the next hour.

I told her how I had stopped off in Chicago for a day on my way East, and how a dozen people had sent their love through me.

'Do they miss me?' she cried ecstatically.

'The whole town is desolate. All the cars have the left rear wheel painted black as a mourning wreath, and there's a persistent wail all night along the North Shore.'

'How gorgeous! Let's go back, Tom. Tomorrow!' Then she added irrelevantly: 'You ought to see the baby.'

'I'd like to.'

'She's asleep. She's three years old. Haven't you ever seen her?'

'Never.'

'Well, you ought to see her. She's—'

Tom Buchanan, who had been hovering restlessly about the room, stopped and rested his hand on my shoulder.

'What you doing, Nick?'

'I'm a bond man.'

'Who with?'

I told him.

'Never heard of them,' he remarked decisively.

This annoyed me.

'You will,' I answered shortly. 'You will if you stay in the East.'

'Oh, I'll stay in the East, don't you worry,' he said, glancing at Daisy and then back at me, as if he were alert for something more. 'I'd be a goddamned fool to live anywhere else.'

At this point Miss Baker said: 'Absolutely!' with such suddenness that I started – it was the first word she had uttered since I came into the room and her voice was surprisingly husky like cigar smoke. Evidently it surprised her as much as it did me, for she yawned and with a series of rapid, deft movements stood up into the room.

'I'm stiff,' she complained, 'I've been lying on that sofa for as long as I can remember.'

I couldn't help my eyes roaming to her chest as she stretched luxuriously and I felt that Tom's did too. Her round, swelling breasts pressed against her dress as she bent her head back and they appeared almost to squeeze her low neckline, as if they were about to overflow. I felt myself go hard and crossed my legs.

'I've been trying to get you to New York all afternoon,' Daisy retorted.

'No, thanks,' said Miss Baker to the four cocktails just in from the pantry, 'I'm absolutely in training.'

Her host looked at her incredulously.

'You are!' He took down his drink as if it were a drop in the bottom of a glass. 'How you ever get anything done is beyond me.'

I looked at Miss Baker again, wondering what it was she 'got done' and just purely glad for a reason to look at her.

Her grey sun-strained eyes looked back at me with polite reciprocal curiosity out of a wan, charming, discontented face. It occurred to me now that I had seen her, or a picture of her, somewhere before.

'You live in West Egg,' she remarked contemptuously. 'I know somebody there.'

'I don't know a single—'

'You must know Gatsby.'

'Gatsby?' demanded Daisy. 'What Gatsby?'

Before I could reply that he was my neighbour, dinner was announced. Wedging his tense arm imperatively under mine, Tom Buchanan compelled me from the room as though he were moving a chequer to another square.

Languidly, their hands set lightly on their hips, the two young women preceded us out on to a rosy-coloured porch, open towards the sunset, where four candles flickered on the table in the diminished wind. Daisy walked like a little girl on a tightrope; delicate and as if at any moment she might fall. Miss Baker, on the other hand, strutted with her deeply curved hips swaying mouth-wateringly. I couldn't keep my eyes off her firm tight behind that pressed the fabric of her dress in the same demanding fashion as her breasts.

'Why candles?' objected Daisy, frowning. She snapped them out with her fingers. 'In two weeks it'll be the longest day in the year.' She looked at us all radiantly. 'Do you always watch for the longest day of the year and then miss it? I always watch for the longest day in the year and then miss it.'

'We ought to plan something,' yawned Miss Baker, sitting down at the table as if she were getting into bed and what a glorious thought that was. I often met women I liked at parties and dinners, of course, but there was something different about Miss Baker. A tenseness hung in the air between us with expectation, and I had never felt anything like it before.

'All right,' said Daisy. 'What'll we plan?' She turned to me helplessly: 'What do people plan?'

Before I could answer her eyes fastened with an awed expression on her little finger.

'Look!' she complained; 'I hurt it.'

We all looked – the knuckle was black and blue.

'You did it, Tom,' she said accusingly. 'I know you didn't mean to, but you did do it. That's what I get for marrying a brute of a man, a great, big, hulking physical specimen of a—'

'I hate that word hulking,' objected Tom crossly, 'even in kidding.'

'Hulking,' insisted Daisy.

Sometimes she and Miss Baker talked at once, unobtrusively and with a bantering inconsequence that was never quite chatter, that was as cool as their white dresses and their impersonal eyes in the absence of all desire. They were here, and they accepted Tom and me, making only a polite pleasant effort to entertain or to be entertained. They knew that presently dinner would be over and a little later the evening too would be over and casually put away. It was sharply different from the West, where an evening was hurried from phase to phase towards its close, in a continually disappointed anticipation or else in sheer nervous dread of the moment itself.

'You make me feel uncivilised, Daisy,' I confessed on my second glass of corky but rather impressive claret. 'Can't you talk about crops or something?'

I meant nothing in particular by this remark, but it was taken up in an unexpected way.

'Civilisation's going to pieces,' broke out Tom violently. 'I've gotten to be a terrible pessimist about things. Have you read *The Rise of the Coloured Empires* by this man Goddard?'

'Why, no,' I answered, rather surprised by his tone.

'Well, it's a fine book, and everybody ought to read it. The idea is if we don't look out the white race will be – will be utterly submerged. It's all scientific stuff; it's been proved.'

'Tom's getting very profound,' said Daisy, with an expression of unthoughtful sadness. 'He reads deep books with long words in them. What was that word we—'

'Well, these books are all scientific,' insisted Tom, glancing at her impatiently. 'This fellow has worked out the whole thing. It's up to us, who are the dominant race, to watch out or these other races will have control of things.'

'We've got to beat them down,' whispered Daisy, winking ferociously towards the fervent sun.

'You ought to live in California—' began Miss Baker, but Tom interrupted her by shifting heavily in his chair.

'This idea is that we're Nordics. I am, and you are, and you are, and –' After an infinitesimal hesitation he included Daisy with a slight nod, and she winked at me again. '– And we've produced all the things that go to make civilisation – oh, science and art, and all that. Do you see?'

There was something pathetic in his concentration, as if his complacency, more acute than of old, was not enough to him any more. When, almost immediately, the telephone rang inside and the butler left the porch Daisy seized upon the momentary interruption and leaned towards me.

'I'll tell you a family secret,' she whispered enthusiastically.

'It's about the butler's nose. Do you want to hear about the butler's nose?'

'That's why I came over tonight.'

'Well, he wasn't always a butler; he used to be the silver polisher for some people in New York that had a silver service for two hundred people. He had to polish it from morning till night, until finally it began to affect his nose—'

'Things went from bad to worse?' suggested Miss Baker in her husky tone.

'Yes. Things went from bad to worse, until finally he had to give up his position.'

For a moment the last sunshine fell with romantic affection upon her glowing face; her voice compelled me forwards breathlessly as I listened – then the glow faded, each light deserting her with lingering regret, like children leaving a pleasant street at dusk.

The butler came back and murmured something close to Tom's ear, whereupon Tom frowned, pushed back his chair, and without a word went inside. As if his absence quickened something within her, Daisy leaned forwards again, her voice glowing and singing.

'I love to see you at my table, Nick. You remind me of a – of a rose, an absolute rose. Doesn't he?' She turned to Miss Baker for confirmation: 'An absolute rose?'

Miss Baker raised an arched brow in my direction and a lazy, indulgent smile spread across her face. 'Yes,' she said. 'An absolute rose.'

This was untrue. I am not even faintly like a rose. Daisy was only extemporising, but a stirring warmth flowed from her, as if her heart was trying to come out to you concealed in one of those breathless, thrilling words. Then suddenly she threw her napkin on the table and excused herself and went into the house.

Miss Baker and I exchanged a short glance consciously devoid of meaning. I was about to speak when she sat up alertly and said 'Sh!' in a warning voice. A subdued impassioned murmur was audible in the room beyond, and Miss Baker leaned forwards unashamed, trying to hear. The murmur trembled on the verge of coherence, sank down, mounted excitedly, and then ceased altogether.

'That Mr Gatsby you spoke of is my neighbour—' I began.

'Don't talk. I want to hear what happens.'

'Is something happening?' I enquired innocently.

'You mean to say you don't know?' said Miss Baker, honestly surprised. 'I thought everybody knew.'

'I don't.'

'Why –' she said hesitantly, 'Tom's got some woman in New York.'

'Got some woman?' I repeated blankly.

Miss Baker nodded.

'She might have the decency not to telephone him at dinnertime. Don't you think?'

I didn't reply and instead chose to stare into her deep grey eyes. I must have stared a little too long and conveyed the direction of my writhing thoughts because her expression suddenly flashed in response.

'They'll be busy for a while,' she said, scraping her chair back like a stretching lioness.

I was not sure what consequence this had, but I felt I ought to speak.

'Would you like to do something in the meantime?' I asked.

She smiled slowly and strutted around the table to my side.

'Yes,' she said simply.

I haltingly stood, jarring the table with my hip, nervous from the blistering heat of her grey eyes and conscious that my erection was obvious from the lump at my crotch. Miss Baker raised her brows and slowly licked her lips, sending my pulse racing and scorching through my body.

'Looks big,' she whispered, leaning forwards and giving me a view down her white dress. I caught the smooth, peach-coloured curve of two breasts and one dark pink flash of an erect nipple. I shivered and the hair on the nape of my neck stood on end.

Miss Baker was evidently younger than me but her burning gaze and velvety voice spoke of a different age of experience. Taking my face in her hands, she pulled me to her and slammed her hot, pillowy lips to mine. I returned the kiss as best I could with what little experience I had, but as she prised my teeth apart with her tongue and stretched it gently into my mouth, I found my senses taking over.

I let my hands glide down her slim torso to the deep arch of her hips and around to her curved behind. I was about to reach up and tentatively touch her breasts when she pulled away from me.

'We don't have long,' she whispered, breathless.

And suddenly she swept down on her knees. I didn't understand until she began unbuttoning my pants.

'But what—'

'It really is big.'

She took my erection in her hands and slowly and gently stroked it.

I gasped and almost bowed over at the electric thrill that surged through my nerves. Quickly I looked at the house to make sure no one was watching.

'It's OK,' she giggled. 'I expect they're having a row.'

Locking her eyes with mine, she flexed her tongue and lightly touched it to the tip of me. I began panting quietly. She did it again, the corners of her mouth lifted in delight; then she puckered her lips into an 'o' and softly sucked.

I couldn't help but groan.

Starting at the base of me, she licked to my tip excruciatingly slowly, her eyes boring into mine. When she reached it, she grated her tongue against it and then sucked me into her mouth whole. Her hands caressed my thighs, stroking the bare skin and sending tendrils of tickling pleasure rushing through my body that had me panting hard.

I flexed my hips into her as she sucked harder and deeper. A fierce punch of pleasure built in my stomach and threatened to overflow. I bit down on my lip as the tension increased, throbbing through my body and making my head dizzy. Suddenly I could take no more and I exploded with release, coming into her mouth in raw, ecstatic delight.

She sighed with bliss and drank me down.

I stepped back, my head still ringing and my body sore from the new, heady experience.

'You had better button up,' she said quietly, standing.

I didn't want to say thank you so I said nothing.

Chapter Three

Jordan Baker was just sitting down when we heard the flutter of a dress and the crunch of leather boots, and Tom and Daisy were back at the table. I sat down quickly as well, blushing a little, but I don't think that they noticed.

Miss Baker barely looked at me for the rest of the evening and if she did, her grey eyes slid over mine without a flicker. I was left high and confused, wondering faintly if I was delusional.

'It couldn't be helped!' cried Daisy with tense gaiety.

She sat down, glanced searchingly at Miss Baker and then at me, and continued: 'I looked outdoors for a minute, and it's very romantic outdoors. There's a bird on the lawn that I think must be a nightingale come over on the Cunard or White Star Line. He's singing away—' Her voice sang: 'It's romantic, isn't it, Tom?'

I wondered then if she had seen us, but she gave no hint of it. She appeared more concerned that we might have overheard her row.

'Very romantic,' said Tom, and then miserably to me: 'If it's light enough after dinner, I want to take you down to the stables.'

The telephone rang inside, startlingly, and as Daisy shook her head decisively at Tom the subject of the stables, in fact all subjects, vanished into air. Among the broken fragments of the last five minutes at table I remember the candles being lit again, pointlessly, and I was conscious of wanting to look squarely at everyone, and yet to avoid all eyes.

The horses, needless to say, were not mentioned again. Tom and Miss Baker, with several feet of twilight between them, strolled back into the library and I watched them go, a little jealous. I wasn't sure what had passed between Miss Baker and me; whether she liked me or was simply bored, and I looked for a similar connection between herself and Tom. Gratifyingly, I saw none, although the wish for such an event was evident in the way that he stared longingly at Miss Baker's tight behind.

After they had disappeared, I followed Daisy around a chain of connecting verandas to the porch in front. In its deep gloom we sat down side by side on a wicker settee and I tried not to think about Miss Baker and listen to my cousin instead.

Daisy took her face in her hands as she spoke, as if feeling its lovely shape, and her eyes moved gradually out into the velvet dusk. I saw that turbulent emotions possessed her, so I asked what I thought would be some sedative questions about her little girl.

'We don't know each other very well, Nick,' she said suddenly. 'Even if we are cousins. You didn't come to my wedding.'

'I wasn't back from the war.'

'That's true.' She hesitated. 'Well, I've had a very bad time, Nick, and I'm pretty cynical about everything.'

Evidently she had reason to be. I waited but she didn't say any more, and after a moment I returned rather feebly to the subject of her daughter.

'I suppose she talks, and – eats, and everything.'

'Oh, yes.' She looked at me absently. 'Listen, Nick; let me tell you what I said when she was born. Would you like to hear?'

'Very much.'

'It'll show you how I've gotten to feel about – things. Well, she was less than an hour old and Tom was God knows where. I woke up out of the ether with an utterly abandoned feeling, and asked the nurse right away if it was a boy or a girl. She told me it was a girl, and so I turned my head away and wept. "All right," I said, "I'm glad it's a girl. And I hope she'll be a fool – that's the best thing a girl can be in this world, a beautiful little fool."

'You see I think everything's terrible anyhow,' she went on in a convinced way. 'Everybody thinks so – the most advanced people. And I know. I've been everywhere and seen everything and done everything.' Her eyes flashed around her in a defiant way, rather like Tom's, and she laughed with thrilling scorn. 'Sophisticated – God, I'm sophisticated!'

The instant her voice broke off, ceasing to compel my attention, my belief, I felt the basic insincerity of what she had said. It made me uneasy, as though the whole evening had been a trick of some sort to exact a contributory emotion from me. I waited, and sure enough, in a moment she looked at me with an absolute smirk on her lovely face, as if she had asserted her membership in a rather distinguished secret society to which she and Tom belonged.

We chatted a little more about nothing at all and then went back in search of the others. Inside, the crimson room bloomed with light.

Tom and Miss Baker sat at either end of the long couch and she read aloud to him from the *Saturday Evening Post* — the words, murmurous and uninflected, running together in a soothing tune. The lamplight, bright on his boots and dull on the cocoa darkness of her hair, glinted along the paper as she turned a page with a flutter of slender muscles in her arms.

When we came in she held us silent for a moment with a lifted hand.

'To be continued,' she said, tossing the magazine on the table with a flourish, 'in our very next issue.'

Her body asserted itself with a restless movement of her knee, and she stood up.

'Ten o'clock,' she remarked, apparently finding the time on the ceiling. 'Time for this good girl to go to bed.'

'Jordan's going to play in the tournament tomorrow,' explained Daisy, 'over at Westchester.'

'Oh – you're Jordan Baker.'

I knew now why her lovely face was familiar – its pleasing contemptuous expression had looked out at me from many rotogravure pictures of the sporting life at Asheville and Hot Springs and Palm Beach. I had heard some story of her too, a critical, unpleasant story, but what it was I had forgotten long ago. I could scarcely believe that I had been sucked by Jordan Baker and I was pretty sure that I had dreamed of such a thing. It seemed practically a dream now anyway since she didn't so much as look at me.

'Goodnight,' she said softly to Daisy. 'Wake me at eight, won't you.'

'If you'll get up.'

'I will. Goodnight, Mr Carraway. See you anon.'

'Of course you will,' confirmed Daisy. 'In fact I think I'll arrange a marriage. Come over often, Nick, and I'll sort of – oh – fling you together. You know – lock you up accidentally in linen closets and push you out to sea in a boat, and all that sort of thing—'

The thought had me quivering with longing in my seat.

'Goodnight,' called Miss Baker from the stairs, her husky voice impersonating a little-girl tone, which was somehow all the more erotic. 'I haven't heard a word.'

'She's a nice girl,' said Tom after a moment. 'They oughtn't to let her run around the country this way.'

'Who oughtn't to?' enquired Daisy coldly.

'Her family.'

'Her family is one aunt about a thousand years old. Besides, Nick's going to look after her, aren't you, Nick? She's going to spend lots of weekends out here this summer. I think the home influence will be very good for her.'

Daisy and Tom looked at each other for a moment in silence.

'Is she from New York?' I asked quickly.

'From Louisville. Our white girlhood was passed together there. Our beautiful white—'

'Did you give Nick a little heart-to-heart talk on the veranda?' demanded Tom suddenly.

'Did I?' She looked at me.

'I can't seem to remember, but I think we talked about the Nordic race. Yes, I'm sure we did. It sort of crept up on us and first thing you know—'

'Don't believe everything you hear, Nick,' he advised me.

I said lightly that I had heard nothing at all, and a few minutes later I got up to go home. They came to the door with me and stood side by side in a cheerful square of light.

I started my motor and sped away, waving to their wisp-like forms as I disappeared.

When I reached my estate at West Egg I ran the car under its shed and sat for a while on an abandoned grass roller in the yard. The wind had blown off, leaving a loud, bright night, with wings beating in the trees and a persistent organ sound as the full bellows of the earth blew the frogs full of life. The silhouette of a moving cat wavered across the moonlight, and turning my head to watch it, I saw that I was not alone – fifty feet away a figure had emerged from the shadow of my neighbour's mansion and was standing with his hands in his pockets regarding the silver pepper of the stars. Something in his leisurely movements and the secure position of his feet upon the lawn suggested that it was Mr Gatsby himself, come out to determine what share was his of our local heavens.

I decided to call to him. Jordan Baker had mentioned him at dinner, and that would do for an introduction; besides I wanted the excuse to say her name aloud to someone, as if she were mine. But I didn't call to him, for he gave a sudden intimation that he was content to be alone – he stretched out his arms towards the dark water in a curious way, and, far as I was from him, I could have sworn he was trembling. Involuntarily I glanced seawards – and distinguished nothing except a single green light, minute and far away, that might have been the end of a dock. When I looked once more for Gatsby he had vanished, and I was alone again in the unquiet darkness, my thoughts turning once more to the beautiful, seductive Jordan Baker whose moans and caresses would haunt me for nights to come.

Chapter Four

About halfway between West Egg and New York the motor road hastily joins the railroad and runs beside it for a quarter of a mile, so as to shrink away from a certain desolate area of land. This is a valley of ashes – a fantastic farm where ashes grow like wheat into ridges and hills and grotesque gardens; where ashes take the forms of houses and chimneys and rising smoke and, finally, with a transcendent effort, of men who move dimly and already crumbling through the powdery air. Occasionally a line of grey cars crawls along an invisible track, gives out a ghastly creak, and comes to rest, and immediately the ash-grey men swarm up with leaden spades and stir up an impenetrable cloud, which screens their obscure operations from your sight. But above the grey land and the spasms of bleak dust which drift endlessly over it, you perceive, after a moment, the eyes of

Dr T. J. Eckleburg. The eyes of Dr T. J. Eckleburg are blue and gigantic – their irises are one yard high. They look out of no face, but, instead, from a pair of enormous yellow spectacles which pass over a nonexistent nose. Evidently some wild wag of an oculist set them there to fatten his practice in the borough of Queens, and then sank down himself into eternal blindness, or forgot them and moved away. But his eyes, dimmed a little by many paintless days, under sun and rain, brood on over the solemn dumping ground.

The valley of ashes is bounded on one side by a small foul river, and, when the drawbridge is up to let barges through, the passengers on waiting trains can stare at the dismal scene for as long as half an hour. There is always a halt there of at least a minute, and it was because of this that I first met Tom Buchanan's mistress.

The fact that he had one was insisted upon wherever he was known. His acquaintances resented the fact that he turned up in popular restaurants with her and, leaving her at a table, sauntered about, chatting with whomsoever he knew. Though I was curious to see her, I had no desire to meet her – but I did. I went up to New York with Tom on the train one afternoon, and when we stopped by the ash heaps he jumped to his feet and, taking hold of my elbow, literally forced me from the car.

'We're getting off,' he insisted. 'I want you to meet my girl.'

I think he'd tanked up a good deal at luncheon, and his determination to have my company bordered on violence. The supercilious assumption was that on a Sunday afternoon I had nothing better to do.

I followed him over a low whitewashed railroad fence, and we walked back a hundred yards along the road under Dr Eckleburg's persistent stare. The only building in sight was a small block of yellow brick sitting on the edge of the wasteland, a sort of compact Main Street ministering to it, and contiguous to absolutely nothing. One of the three shops it contained was for rent and another was an all-night restaurant, approached by a trail of ashes; the third was a garage – Repairs. George B. Wilson. Cars bought and sold. – and I followed Tom inside.

The interior was unprosperous and bare; the only car visible was the dust-covered wreck of a Ford which crouched in a dim corner. It had occurred to me that this shadow of a garage must be a blind, and that sumptuous and romantic apartments were concealed overhead, when the proprietor himself appeared in the door of an office, wiping his hands on a piece of waste. He was a blond, spiritless man, anaemic, and faintly handsome. When he saw us a damp gleam of hope sprang into his light blue eyes.

'Hello, Wilson, old man,' said Tom, slapping him jovially on the shoulder. 'How's business?'

'I can't complain,' answered Wilson unconvincingly. 'When are you going to sell me that car?'

'Next week; I've got my man working on it now.'

'Works pretty slow, don't he?'

'No, he doesn't,' said Tom coldly. 'And if you feel that way about it, maybe I'd better sell it somewhere else after all.'

'I don't mean that,' explained Wilson quickly. 'I just meant—'

His voice faded off and Tom glanced impatiently around the garage. Then I heard footsteps on a stairs, and in a moment the thickish figure of a woman blocked out the light from the office door. She was in the middle thirties, and faintly stout, but she carried her surplus flesh sensuously as some women can. Her face, above a spotted dress of dark blue crêpe-de-Chine, contained no facet or gleam of beauty, but there was an immediately perceptible vitality about her as if the nerves of her body were continually smouldering. She smiled slowly and, walking through her husband as if he were a ghost, shook hands with Tom, looking him flush in the eye. Then she wet her lips, and without turning around spoke to her husband in a soft, coarse voice:

'Get some chairs, why don't you, so somebody can sit down.'

'Oh, sure,' agreed Wilson hurriedly, and went towards the little office, mingling immediately with the cement colour of the walls. A white ashen dust veiled his dark suit and his pale hair as it veiled everything in the vicinity – except his wife, who moved close to Tom.

'I want to see you,' said Tom intently. 'Get on the next train.'

'All right.'

'I'll meet you by the news-stand on the lower level.' She nodded and moved away from him just as George Wilson emerged with two chairs from his office door.

Half an hour later, we waited for her down the road and out of sight. It was a few days before the Fourth of July, and a grey, scrawny Italian child was setting torpedoes in a row along the railroad track.

'Terrible place, isn't it,' said Tom, exchanging a frown with Dr Eckleburg.

'Awful.'

'It does her good to get away.'

'Doesn't her husband object?'

'Wilson? He thinks she goes to see her sister in New York. He's so dumb he doesn't know he's alive.'

So Tom Buchanan and his girl and I went up together to New York – or not quite together, for Mrs Wilson sat discreetly in another car. Tom deferred that much to the sensibilities of those East Eggers who might be on the train.

She had changed her dress to a brown figured muslin, which stretched tight over her rather wide hips as Tom helped her to the platform in New York. At the news-stand she bought a copy of *Town Tattle* and a moving-picture magazine, and in the station drugstore some cold cream and a small flask of perfume. Upstairs, in the solemn echoing drive she let four taxicabs drive away before she selected a new one, lavender-coloured with grey upholstery, and in this we slid out from the mass of the station into the glowing sunshine. But immediately she turned sharply from the window and, leaning forwards, tapped on the front glass.

'I want to get one of those dogs,' she said earnestly. 'I want to get one for the apartment. They're nice to have – a dog.'

We backed up to a grey old man who bore an absurd resemblance to John D. Rockefeller. In a basket swung from

his neck cowered a dozen very recent puppies of an inde-
terminate breed.

'What kind are they?' asked Mrs Wilson eagerly, as he
came to the taxi-window.

'All kinds. What kind do you want, lady?'

'I'd like to get one of those police dogs; I don't suppose
you got that kind?'

The man peered doubtfully into the basket, plunged in
his hand and drew one up, wriggling, by the back of the
neck.

'That's no police dog,' said Tom.

'No, it's not exactly a police dog,' said the man with disappointment in his voice. 'It's more of an Airedale.' He
passed his hand over the brown washrag of a back. 'Look at
that coat. Some coat. That's a dog that'll never bother you
with catching cold.'

'I think it's cute,' said Mrs Wilson enthusiastically. 'How
much is it?'

'That dog?' He looked at it admiringly. 'That dog will
cost you ten dollars.'

The Airedale – undoubtedly there was an Airedale concerned in it somewhere, though its feet were startlingly
white – changed hands and settled down into Mrs Wilson's
lap, where she fondled the weatherproof coat with rapture.

'Is it a boy or a girl?' she asked delicately.

'That dog? That dog's a boy.'

'It's a bitch,' said Tom decisively. 'Here's your money. Go and buy ten more dogs with it.'

We drove over to Fifth Avenue, so warm and soft, almost pastoral, on the summer Sunday afternoon that I wouldn't have been surprised to see a great flock of white sheep turn the corner.

'Hold on,' I said, 'I have to leave you here.'

'No, you don't,' interposed Tom quickly.

'Myrtle'll be hurt if you don't come up to the apartment. Won't you, Myrtle?'

'Come on,' she urged. 'I'll telephone my sister Catherine. She's said to be very beautiful by people who ought to know.'

'Well, I'd like to, but—'

We went on, cutting back again over the Park towards the West Hundreds. At 158th Street the cab stopped at one slice in a long white cake of apartment houses. Throwing a regal homecoming glance around the neighbourhood, Mrs Wilson gathered up her dog and her other purchases, and went haughtily in.

'I'm going to have the McKees come up,' she announced as we rose in the elevator. 'And, of course, I got to call up my sister, too.'

The apartment was on the top floor – a small living room, a small dining room, a small bedroom, and a bath. The living room was crowded to the doors with a set of tapestried furniture entirely too large for it, so that to move about was to stumble continually over scenes of ladies swinging in the gardens of Versailles. The only picture was an over-enlarged photograph, apparently a hen sitting on a blurred rock. Looked at from a distance, however, the hen resolved itself into a bonnet, and the countenance of a stout old lady beamed down into the room. Several old copies of *Town Tattle* lay on the table together with a copy of *Simon Called Peter*, and some of the small scandal magazines of Broadway. Mrs Wilson was first concerned with the dog. A reluctant elevator-boy went for a box full of straw and some milk, to which he added on his own initiative a tin of large, hard dog biscuits – one of which decomposed apathetically in the saucer of milk all afternoon. Meanwhile Tom brought out a bottle of whiskey from a locked bureau door.

I have been drunk just twice in my life, and the second time was that afternoon; so everything that happened has a dim, hazy cast over it, although until after eight o'clock the apartment was full of cheerful sun. Sitting on Tom's lap Mrs Wilson called up several people on the telephone; then there were no cigarettes, and I went out to buy some at the drugstore on the corner. When I came back they had disappeared, so I sat down discreetly in the living room and read a chapter of *Simon Called Peter*. Either it was terrible stuff or the whiskey distorted things, because it didn't make any sense to me and I was continually disturbed by shrieks, grunts and luxurious groans from another room. I tried to block them out, but they rippled through me, bringing back my memories of Jordan. I'd thought of her obsessively in the intervening time without a hope of seeing her again. I woke at night panting for her and remembering the feel of her mouth on me. I desperately wanted to touch her again and feel her contemptuous, aloof expression burn my skin. I'd made enquiries and even phoned Daisy, but my efforts had reaped no results. Either she was avoiding me or it was just bad luck.

Just as Tom and Myrtle (after the first drink Mrs Wilson and I called each other by our first names) reappeared, company commenced to arrive at the apartment door and I was thankfully given some distraction.

The first guest, Mr McKee, was a pale, feminine man from the flat below. He had just shaved, for there was a white spot of lather on his cheekbone, and he was most respectful in his greeting to everyone in the room. He informed me that he was in the 'artistic game' and I gathered later that he was a photographer and had made the dim enlargement of Mrs Wilson's mother which hovered like an ectoplasm on the wall. His wife was shrill, languid, handsome, and horrible. She told me with pride that her husband had photographed her a hundred and twenty-seven times since they had been married.

The sister of Myrtle, Catherine, was a voluptuous, worldly girl of about thirty, with a solid, sticky bob of red hair, and a complexion powdered milky white. Her eyebrows had been plucked and then drawn on again at a more rakish angle, but the efforts of nature towards the restoration of the old alignment gave a blurred air to her face. When she moved about there was an incessant clicking as innumerable pottery bracelets jingled up and down upon her arms. She came in with such a proprietary haste, and looked around so possessively at the furniture that I wondered if she lived here. But when I asked her she laughed immoderately, repeated my question aloud, and told me she lived with a girlfriend at a hotel. Then, checking that she was not watched by others, she snaked her hand about my back and brushed her fingertips across my groin, making me jump. She tossed her sticky red bob of hair in a furtive attempt at coquettishness and winked theatrically before turning away.

Mrs Wilson had changed her costume some time before, and was now attired in an elaborate afternoon dress of cream-coloured chiffon, which gave out a continual rustle as she swept about the room. With the influence of the dress her personality had also undergone a change. The intense vitality that had been so remarkable in the garage was converted into impressive hauteur. Her laughter, her gestures, her assertions became more violently affected moment by moment, and as she expanded the room grew smaller around her, until she seemed to be revolving on a noisy, creaking pivot through the smoky air.

'My dear,' she told her sister in a high, mincing shout, 'most of these fellas will cheat you every time. All they think of is money. I had a woman up here last week to look at my feet, and when she gave me the bill you'd of thought she had my appendicitis out.'

'What was the name of the woman?' asked Mrs McKee.

'Mrs Eberhardt. She goes around looking at people's feet in their own homes.'

'I like your dress,' remarked Mrs McKee, 'I think it's adorable.'

Mrs Wilson rejected the compliment by raising her eyebrow in disdain.

'It's just a crazy old thing,' she said. 'I just slip it on sometimes when I don't care what I look like.'

'But it looks wonderful on you, if you know what I mean,' pursued Mrs McKee. 'If Chester could only get you in that pose I think he could make something of it.'

We all looked in silence at Mrs Wilson, who removed a strand of hair from over her eyes and looked back at us with a brilliant smile. Mr McKee regarded her intently with his head on one side, and then moved his hand back and forth slowly in front of his face.

'I should change the light,' he said after a moment. 'I'd like to bring out the modelling of the features. And I'd try to get hold of all the back hair.'

'I wouldn't think of changing the light,' cried Mrs McKee. 'I think it's—'

Her husband said 'Sh!' and we all looked at the subject again, whereupon Tom Buchanan yawned audibly and got to his feet.

'You McKees have something to drink,' he said. 'Get some more ice and mineral water, Myrtle, before everybody goes to sleep.'

'I told that boy about the ice.' Myrtle raised her eyebrows in despair at the shiftlessness of the lower orders. 'These people! You have to keep after them all the time.'

She looked at me and laughed pointlessly. Then she flounced over to the dog, kissed it with ecstasy, and swept into the kitchen, implying that a dozen chefs awaited her orders there.

'I've done some nice things out on Long Island,' asserted Mr McKee.

Tom looked at him blankly.

'Two of them we have framed downstairs.'

'Two what?' demanded Tom.

'Two studies. One of them I call *Montauk Point – The Gulls*, and the other I call *Montauk Point – The Sea*.'

The sister Catherine sat down beside me on the couch.

'Do you live down on Long Island, too?' she enquired, batting her lashes and pouting her lips at me.

'I live at West Egg.'

'Really? I was down there at a party about a month ago. At a man named Gatsby's. Do you know him?'

'I live next door to him.'

'Well, they say he's a nephew or a cousin of Kaiser Wilhelm's. That's where all his money comes from.'

'Really?'

She nodded.

'I'm scared of him. I'd hate to have him get anything on me.'

This absorbing information about my neighbour was interrupted by Mrs McKee's pointing suddenly at Catherine:

'Chester, I think you could do something with her,' she broke out, but Mr McKee only nodded in a bored way, and turned his attention to Tom.

'I'd like to do more work on Long Island, if I could get the entry. All I ask is that they should give me a start.'

'Ask Myrtle,' said Tom, breaking into a short shout of laughter as Mrs Wilson entered with a tray. 'She'll give you a letter of introduction, won't you Myrtle?'

'Do what?' she asked, startled.

'You'll give McKee a letter of introduction to your husband, so he can do some studies of him.' His lips moved silently for a moment as he invented. '*George B. Wilson at the Gasoline Pump*, or something like that.'

Catherine leaned close to me, pressing her motherly chest to mine, and whispered in my ear: 'Neither of them can stand the person they're married to.'

'Can't they?'

'Can't stand them.' She looked at Myrtle and then at Tom. 'What I say is, why go on living with them if they can't stand them? If I was them I'd get a divorce and get married to each other right away.'

'Doesn't she like Wilson either?'

The answer to this was unexpected. It came from Myrtle, who had overheard the question, and it was violent and obscene.

'You see,' cried Catherine triumphantly. She lowered her voice again. 'It's really his wife that's keeping them apart. She's a Catholic, and they don't believe in divorce.'

Daisy was not a Catholic, and I was a little shocked at the elaborateness of the lie.

'When they do get married,' continued Catherine, 'they're going West to live for a while until it blows over.' She began gliding seamlessly to the door and I found myself following her.

'It'd be more discreet to go to Europe,' I replied, barely registering as we walked out into the hallway.

'Oh, do you like Europe?' Catherine exclaimed surprisingly, pushing a bedroom door open. 'I just got back from Monte Carlo.'

'Really.'

'Just last year. I went over there with another girl.'

'Stay long?'

'No, we just went to Monte Carlo and back. We went by way of Marseilles. We had over twelve hundred dollars when we started, but we got gypped out of it all in two days in the private rooms. We had an awful time getting back, I can tell you. God, how I hated that town!'

She was standing in the empty, shadowed bedroom, waiting for me to follow. The room was simple and plain, much like Catherine herself, and I erred in the doorway, fighting the urge of my aching desire and the memory of Jordan Baker.

Had I not followed Catherine out of the other room, secretly knowing that this was where we were headed? My erection was throbbing intensely, begging for relief. The whiskey fuzzed my brain and increased the tendrils of cutting desire that beat through my body. Behind Catherine's form, I could see a bed with rumpled sheets and I guessed that this was the location of the grunts, groans and moans I had heard earlier. At the thought, a scorching jerk of desire flooded my body and I stumbled into the room.

Catherine smiled at me, reaching out her thick arms and running the tips of her fingers lightly down my chest. In return, I grasped one of her large breasts, surprised that although not pert like Jordan's, it was rounded and soft and nice all the same.

While I fondled her breasts with gentle, slow circles across the silky fabric of her dress, Catherine tipped back her head and groaned softly, leaning her pelvis against my hips. I pulsed into the curve of her thighs and squeezed her hard in eagerness, feeling her bend into me.

Locking her fingers behind my head, she brought her lips to mine and kissed me, hard and slow. My breath hitched in my throat as she suddenly bit down on my lip before sucking and smoothing it better with her tongue. Aroused, I moved my hands behind her, to the large curves of her buttocks. Deep waves of burning desire rippled through me and pricked the pit of my stomach as we licked, sucked and kissed one another.

Catherine pulled away gasping, and I saw her eyes, glazed with yearning, run appraisingly down my body. In a deft, smooth movement, she tugged her dress over her head and stood naked except for her heeled shoes and panties. The silky material pooled beside her and the shadowed light of the room highlighted the contours of her voluptuous body. Naked, her red hair illuminated the lily-whiteness of her skin and her large breasts curved beautifully against the soft fleshiness of her chest. Her thighs were thick and smooth and inviting – her stomach was curved and led a seductive undulation to the warmth between her legs.

My erection was pounding in return, and my groin impatiently ached for relief. Seeing my yearning, Catherine smiled seductively and slowly brought one finger up to her mouth, biting it gently between her white teeth. Then she sucked and licked the tip, her penetrating gaze never leaving mine.

I reached out for her and grasped the smooth, soft flesh of her wide hips, burying my fingernails into it. She grasped back and pressed herself against my chest, gasping again and again into my ear and tickling my neck with her warm breath. Unable to bare it, I ran my hands around to her behind and squeezed the succulent roundness of her cheeks.

Moaning into my neck she began unbuttoning my shirt, pulling fervently at the stiff fabric. One button snapped off and fell to the floor before I felt her hands slide beneath the material and caress my pecs and torso with sleek strokes, leaving a burning trail of prickling craving across my skin. Her fingers snaked down to my stomach, and then further, tugging gently at the track of hair that dipped lower.

I gasped as she began hurriedly tearing off my pants. In a raw frenzy, I raked my fingers through her hair and she dragged her nails down my thighs, forcing a further thick heat of longing to curdle in my groin. Throwing off my pants, I pushed her on to the bed and she lay back, knotting the sheets into her fists and curling her legs around my torso to pull me closer.

Bending over her, I traced kisses across her neck, nipping and sucking the skin, before moving back to her mouth. I traced her Cupid's bow with the tip of my tongue, then pushed it between her wet lips and licked the walls of her cheeks. Catherine moaned and writhed as I began again and pulled down my underwear, reaching for my erection, which she tickled, tantalising me.

She began moving her hands up in smooth, hard strokes and I felt a well of lust collect in my stomach – a fiery friction that intensified slowly. She tugged and pulled me closer so that I pulsed across her breasts while she rubbed and stroked it faster and faster. The pressure inside me built further and further as she tugged me yet harder and faster and then suddenly I came in a punch of pleasure, coming across the white tender skin of her breasts which dribbled over her décolletage and trickled across her neck. I panted slowly, my mind still foggy with whiskey.

'My turn,' she said with a lazy smile.

I moved my hands across the creamy flesh of her tummy, creeping beneath her legs before a sound interrupted us.

'Catherine?'

Chapter Five

It was Myrtle and we both jumped up, hurriedly pulling on our clothes.

'Catherine?' her sister called again and the door slid open.

Myrtle stood on the threshold, barely containing a smirk. 'Don't you like it?' she asked after a tense second of silence where she glanced at each of us, relishing our unease. 'I furnished this room myself. Come on back to the party, Catherine, we're waiting for you.' She giggled and stepped away from the door.

Straightening out her hair Catherine winked and me and mouthed, 'Later.'

But there would be no later; I would soon sink into a drunken haze in which I would be little use to myself let alone anyone else. However then I was still in a blurred state of pleasure so I followed the women back into the other room.

The late afternoon sky bloomed in the window for a moment like the blue honey of the Mediterranean – then the shrill voice of Mrs McKee called my attention.

'I almost made a mistake, too,' she declared vigorously. 'I almost married a little kike who'd been after me for years. I knew he was below me. Everybody kept saying to me: "Lucille, that man's way below you!" But if I hadn't met Chester, he'd of got me sure.'

'Yes, but listen,' said Myrtle, nodding her head up and down, 'at least you didn't marry him.'

'I know I didn't.'

'Well, I married him,' said Myrtle, ambiguously. 'And that's the difference between your case and mine.'

'Why did you, Myrtle?' asked Catherine drily, evidently angry that her sister had disturbed us. 'Nobody forced you to.'

Myrtle considered.

'I married him because I thought he was a gentleman,' she said finally. 'I thought he knew something about breed-ing, but he wasn't fit to lick my shoe.'

'You were crazy about him for a while,' pointed out Catherine, almost determined to show her sister up.

'Crazy about him!' cried Myrtle incredulously. 'Who said

I was crazy about him? I never was any more crazy about him than I was about that man there.'

She pointed suddenly at me, and everyone looked at me accusingly. I tried to show by my expression that I had played no part in her past.

'The only crazy I was was when I married him. I knew right away I made a mistake. He borrowed somebody's best suit to get married in, and never even told me about it, and the man came after it one day when he was out. "Oh, is that your suit?" I said, "this is the first I ever heard about it." But I gave it to him and then I lay down and cried to beat the band all afternoon.'

The bottle of whiskey – a second one – was now in constant demand by all present, excepting Catherine, who 'felt just as good on nothing at all'. Tom rang for the janitor and sent him for some celebrated sandwiches, which were a complete supper in themselves. I wanted to get out and walk southwards towards the park through the soft twilight and ease my drunkenness, but each time I tried to go I became entangled in some wild, strident argument which pulled me back, as if with ropes, into my chair. Yet high over the city our line of yellow windows must have contributed their share of human secrecy to the casual watcher in the darkening streets, and I was him too, looking up and wondering. I was within and without, simultaneously enchanted and repelled by the inexhaustible variety of life.

Catherine kept winking at me throughout the night and it quickly got tiring. Everyone could see and Tom was making a great joke of it. I wished she'd stop. After another come-hither look in my direction, Myrtle suddenly pushed past her sister and pulled her chair close to mine. Her warm breath poured over me the story of her first meeting with Tom and I was actually glad of the distraction.

'It was on the two little seats facing each other that are always the last ones left on the train. I was going up to New York to see my sister and spend the night. He had on a dress suit and patent leather shoes, and I couldn't keep my eyes off him, but every time he looked at me I had to pretend to be looking at the advertisement over his head. When we came into the station he was next to me, and his white shirt-front pressed against my arm, and so I told him I'd have to call a policeman, but he knew I lied. I was so excited that when I got into a taxi with him I didn't hardly know I wasn't getting into a subway train. All I kept think-ing about, over and over, was "You can't live for ever; you can't live for ever."'

She turned to Mrs McKee and the room rang full of her artificial laughter.

'My dear,' she cried, 'I'm going to give you this dress as soon as I'm through with it. I've got to get another one tomorrow. I'm going to make a list of all the things I've got to get. A massage and a wave, and a collar for the dog, and one of those cute little ashtrays where you touch a spring, and a wreath with a black silk bow for Mother's grave that'll last all summer. I got to write down a list so I won't forget all the things I got to do.'

Mrs McKee nodded vaguely before lurching away.

Myrtle moved back to me. She suddenly leaned in close so that her large form was pressed against my knee.

'Fancy stepping out to the bedroom?' she whispered.

Despite the drunken haze of the whiskey, I jumped slightly and looked at Tom who was turned away.

'He won't notice us gone for just a minute, what do you say?'

I felt sick.

'I'm better than my sister,' she hissed when I didn't answer. 'I can promise you that. I'm better. How do you think I keep Tom happy, I'm—'

Thankfully he heard his name and he moved over to us.

'What's this?'

'We were talking about you,' Myrtle replied, looking up at him through flashing eyes.

He glanced at me and smiled.

It was nine o'clock – almost immediately afterwards I looked at my watch and found it was ten. Mr McKee was asleep on a chair with his fists clenched in his lap, like a photograph of a man of action. Taking out my handkerchief I wiped from his cheek the remains of the spot of dried lather that had worried me all the afternoon.

The little dog was sitting on the table looking with blind eyes through the smoke, and from time to time groaning faintly. Catherine was still winking at me but I was now too drunk to notice. People disappeared, reappeared, made plans to go somewhere, and then lost each other, searched for each other, found each other a few feet away. Some time towards midnight Tom and Myrtle stood face to face discussing, in impassioned voices, whether Mrs Wilson had any right to mention Daisy's name.

'Daisy! Daisy! Daisy!' shouted Myrtle. 'I'll say it whenever I want to! Daisy! Dai—'

Making a short deft movement, Tom broke her nose with his open hand.

Then there were bloody towels upon the bathroom floor, and women's voices scolding, and high over the confusion a long broken wail of pain. Mr McKee awoke from his doze and started in a daze towards the door. When he had gone halfway he turned around and stared at the scene – his wife and Catherine scolding and consoling as they stumbled here and there among the crowded furniture with articles of aid, and the despairing figure on the couch, bleeding fluently, and trying to spread a copy of *Town Tattle* over the tapestry scenes of Versailles. Then Mr McKee turned and continued on out the door. Taking my hat from the chandelier, I followed.

'Come to lunch some day,' he suggested, as we groaned down in the elevator.

'Where?'

'Anywhere.'

'Keep your hands off the lever,' snapped the elevator boy.

'I beg your pardon,' said Mr McKee with dignity, 'I didn't know I was touching it.'

'All right,' I agreed, 'I'll be glad to.'

. . . I was standing beside his bed and he was sitting up between the sheets, clad in his underwear, with a great portfolio in his hands.

'*Beauty and the Beast . . . Loneliness . . . Old Grocery Horse . . . Brook'n Bridge . . .*'

Then I was lying half asleep in the cold lower level of the Pennsylvania Station, staring at the morning *Tribune*, and waiting for the four o'clock train.

Chapter Six

There were always strange noises from my neighbour's house through the summer nights – soft music, shrieks, groans and wails of ecstasy. In his blue gardens men and girls came and went like moths among the whisperings and the champagne and the stars. At high tide in the afternoon I watched his guests diving from the tower of his raft, or scantily clad taking the sun on the hot sand of his beach while his two motor boats slit the waters of the Sound, drawing aquaplanes over cataracts of foam. On weekends his Rolls-Royce became an omnibus, bearing parties to and from the city between nine in the morning and long past midnight, while his station wagon scampered like a brisk yellow bug to meet all trains. And on Mondays eight servants, including an extra gardener, toiled all day with mops and scrubbing brushes and hammers and garden shears, repairing the ravages of the night before.

Every Friday five crates of oranges and lemons arrived from a fruitier in New York – every Monday these same oranges and lemons left his back door in a pyramid of pulpless halves. There was a machine in the kitchen which could extract the juice of two hundred oranges in half an hour if a little button was pressed two hundred times by a butler's thumb.

At least once a fortnight a corps of caterers came down with several hundred feet of canvas and enough coloured lights to make a Christmas tree of Gatsby's enormous garden. On buffet tables, garnished with glistening horsd'oeuvres, spiced baked hams crowded against salads of harlequin designs and pastry pigs and turkeys bewitched to a dark gold. In the main hall a bar with a real brass rail was set up, and stocked with gins and liquors and with cordials so long forgotten that most of his female guests were too young to know one from another.

By seven o'clock the orchestra has arrived, no thin fivepiece affair, but a whole pitful of oboes and trombones and saxophones and viols and cornets and piccolos, and low and high drums. The last swimmers have come in from the beach now and are dressing upstairs; the cars from New York are parked five deep in the drive, and already the halls and salons and verandas are gaudy with primary colours, and hair shorn in strange new ways, and shawls beyond the dreams of Castile. The bar is in full swing, and floating rounds of cocktails permeate the garden outside, until the air is alive with chatter, laughter and carnal grunts and introductions forgotten on the spot, and enthusiastic meetings between women who never knew each other's names.

The lights grow brighter as the earth lurches away from the sun, and now the orchestra is playing yellow cocktail music, and the opera of voices pitches a key higher. Laughter is easier minute by minute, spilled with prodigality, tipped out at a cheerful word. The groups change more swiftly, swell with new arrivals, dissolve and form in the same breath; already there are wanderers, confident girls who weave here and there among the stouter and more stable, become for a sharp, joyous moment the centre of a group, and then, excited with triumph, glide on through the sea-change of faces and voices and colour under the constantly changing light.

Suddenly one of the gypsies, in trembling opal, seizes a cocktail out of the air, dumps it down for courage and, moving her hands like Frisco, dances out alone on the canvas platform. A momentary hush; the orchestra leader varies his rhythm obligingly for her, and there is a burst of chatter as the erroneous news goes around that she is Gilda Gray's understudy from the Follies. The party has begun.

I believe that on the first night I went to Gatsby's house I was one of the few guests who had actually been invited. People were not invited – they went there. They got into automobiles which bore them out to Long Island, and somehow they ended up at Gatsby's door. Once there they were introduced by somebody who knew Gatsby, and after that they conducted themselves according to the rules of behaviour associated with amusement parks. Sometimes they came and went without having met Gatsby at all, they came for the party with a simplicity of heart that was its own ticket of admission.

I had actually been invited. A chauffeur in a uniform of robin's-egg blue crossed my lawn early that Saturday morning with a surprisingly formal note from his employer: the honour would be entirely Gatsby's, it said, if I would attend his 'little party' that night. He had seen me several times, and had intended to call on me long before, but a peculiar combination of circumstances had prevented it – signed Jay Gatsby, in a majestic hand. I wanted to go purely to finally meet this fantastical figure, but another part of me thought that Jordan Baker might be there, the other part that had not forgotten her pillowy lips and large, full breasts.

Dressed up in white flannels I went over to his lawn a little after seven, and wandered up to the grand front entrance. The grounds of the mansion were deserted and I would have assumed I was too early had I not already watched streams of guests entering, their slick motor cars purring into the driveway. I pondered the possibility that my arrival might be interrupting some speech or event. Perhaps I was late? But there had not been a time specified on the invitation.

The grounds were eerily empty. The band was playing around the back, on the lawn, but otherwise there was no one. I had not expected this, thinking instead that I would be sucked into a void of vacant, joyful people littering the space like bejewelled leeches.

I rang the bell and stood on the vast porch in the darkening evening, listening to the crooning of the band. After my call had gone unanswered for several minutes, I rang the bell again, but still no one came. I began to worry and tug at the collar of my shirt, thinking that I could have done all number of things wrong and feeling that Gatsby and all his monstrous guests were laughing at my expense, somewhere high up in one of the mansion's glazed windows.

After my third call had gone unanswered, rather than retreat, I pushed open one of the double doors and shuffled inside. The hall was decadent, as I had anticipated, but it was also empty. I peered around, thinking that maybe I had misread the date, time or whole invitation. I was just beginning to lose my nerve and consider turning back when I heard a gasp of joy.

The hallway was dimly lit by a gilded chandelier and the gasp had come from behind a door on my left. It had had such lustful undertones that a shiver had coursed down my body and the hair at the nape of my neck tingled. I stared at the door, bathed in golden shadow, my heart thudding in my chest, fighting the urgent desire to know what was on the other side.

I glanced around the hallway once more, wondering if anyone would appear, but it remained deserted. My feet shuffled closer to the door, my curiosity mounting, and an itch of desire formed in the pit of my stomach. I stood in front of it, beads of sweat congealing on my brow. From behind the door there was the sound of an ecstatic shriek and an accompanying deep, satisfied laugh. Unable to stop myself, I reached forwards and gently pushed the door open . . .

I started back from the scene in shock. My eyes were

greeted with the partial view of knotted, writhing limbs and ecstatic, pleasured faces. Skin was bare and brown; tanned from the day sunbathing in Gatsby's gardens, and the air was filled with fervent groans and deep grunts. The atmosphere was carnal and lustful and shameless. There must have been six or seven men and women in there, grasping, thrusting and caressing on the Persian rug. They didn't notice my intrusion or, if they did, then they did not pause in their cavorting.

It was too much for me. I fled from the scene, fled from the thought, fled through the mansion, not knowing where I was going. As I ran, I saw more closed doors and I am sure I heard shrieks and groans and moans and cries of desire. Gatsby's infamous parties became all too clear to me now and it was too much. I stumbled through ornate lounges until I found my way to the porch and just as I burst out into the cool evening air, I spied a discarded brown plaited horsewhip.

I ran outside, my heart pounding and my erection stiff against my leg. I was terrified and allured all at once. The writhing bodies pulsed through my mind and I could still hear the convulsive moans of pleasure and see the crimson blindfolds strapped across burning eyes and bound wrists. Every naked body in there had seemed so alive; so full of electric, pulsing thrills. It sent waves of yearning through my body that spiked my stomach and made me consider, albeit briefly, returning.

Keen to calm my thudding chest, I walked down a flight of marble steps and into the gardens. The sound of the band lulled me and I listened to its gentle waving melody as I wandered about the ornamented greenery. I was faintly surprised to see that even Gatsby's plant pots were gilded. I almost drank from one of the many statuesque fountains, wondering if it spouted some sort of elixir.

I had just completed a full circle, exploring the left flank of Gatsby's gardens and trying to quell the image of two women entwined around a man, when Jordan Baker appeared. She stood on the marble steps, leaning a little backwards and looking down with contemptuous interest. Her arrival stopped my breath and quickened my heartbeat all at once. It was exactly what I had hoped for.

'Hello!' I called, advancing towards her, the thrills of the evening making me bold.

We were alone together except for the band.

'I thought you might be here,' she responded absently as I came up, not a bit surprised.

She was wearing a long, black dress of liquid silk without any underwear. It grazed her large, plump breasts, hugged her curved hips and slid between her legs as she stood with them slightly apart. The dark evening made her grey eyes darker, like smoke on a lake at midnight, and their cat-like slant gave her a dreamy gaze.

'You hoped to meet me here then?' I asked, very hopeful myself that this was the case.

She turned her dreamy gaze on me and shrugged slowly.

My breath was tearing from my throat in hurried gasps now and the bulge in my pants was evident. I hurriedly tried to hide it by moving sideways but she stopped me, stepping forwards and taking it in her grasp.

My body froze with tight anticipation and I suddenly wondered what Jordan Baker had been doing in the mansion before she followed me out here. Had she been one of those writhing bodies? From the way her eyes confidently and bluntly blazed into mine, I assumed she had.

'I saw you leave in there,' she whispered in her husky tone, tilting her head so that she was breathing gently into my ear and the hairs on my neck were tingling. 'Why did you go?'

I couldn't reply.

'You weren't scared were you?' she added.

I swallowed hard and resisted the urge to caress the front of her silky dress.

She smiled and moved even closer, pressing her breasts up against my chest. I could smell the heady, sweet scent of her perfume and I could see that her brow was slightly damp from the warmth inside the mansion. I could even lightly feel the slow, soft thud of her heartbeat.

'I was surprised . . . by what I saw inside,' I gasped at last.

She raised her eyebrows. 'Didn't you want to join in?' She squeezed my balls a little tighter.

I couldn't reply.

Fondling them in her hands, she teased me. 'Shall we go inside?' she asked, one corner of her full lips tugging upwards in a suggestive grin.

I nodded.

Allowing me to take her slender, golden arm, she guided me back into the warm glow of the mansion. I should have been nervous, but I could only think of Jordan. The air was filled with moans and cries of ecstasy that sent shudders down my spine and I was just considering how I would fare in the knot of writhing, naked bodies when Jordan pulled me towards a different door.

She swung it open carelessly and I was surprised to see an empty, simply furnished room. There was a long soft couch in the middle, a few bookcases dotted about and an air of quiet solitude.

'I think we need a little privacy,' she whispered, shutting the door.

I was relieved and my cutting throbs of desire quickened as she led me to the couch. I would prefer it if it was just the two of us; I wanted Jordan Baker all to myself.

She began tugging at my jacket and shirt feverishly. The memory of our last meeting flickered through my mind as I promptly tore them off and I received a sweet clench of my stomach muscles to remind me of the delight her tongue had wreaked. I scarcely knew what to expect now and my head rang with the rhythmic beat of my pulse.

I longed to see her bare breasts and her naked hips. I wanted to run my hands over them and feel her warm, strong legs wrapped around my waist. At Yale, friends had often hinted that I should go downtown to alleviate myself of my 'problem', but I had never found the gaudy night-women appealing. I should have been nervous with Jordan now, but she was so self-assured and enticing that carnal instinct overwhelmed me. I barely registered that this was the monumental moment when I would lose my virginity, but I later revelled in my choice of partner. I was glad that I had not heeded the advice of my Yale peers. Jordan was succulent and fresh and, despite circumstances, she had a subtle hint of naivety that was incredibly appealing.

As I threw my shirt on the floor, she pulled my head down to her and kissed me hard. Her lips were fiery and soft. She slipped her tongue into my mouth and let it revolve in tiny circles against the walls of my cheeks while she ran her claw-like nails across my stomach and chest, leaving me quivering and clutching at her desperately.

'You must play sport,' she gasped, pulling away from me and looking admiringly at my bare torso. She ran a finger down the tufts of hair from my navel to my waistband.

I slid the straps of her dress from her shoulders and let it fall in a black pooled heap of night sky on the carpeted floor. She squeaked slightly at the cool air on her naked body, but I scarcely heard since my eyes were roaming all over her with a hot, intense gaze.

Her body was just as I had imagined it: toned, curved and smooth. Her large, pert breasts nipped into a slim, smooth waist, which arched into her wide hips. Her legs were muscular, her feet delicate and her skin was the beautiful tawny shade of the wealthy. I could not have imagined Jordan Baker better. She was beautiful and seductive and I wanted her.

Unable to stop myself, I pulled her into my arms and began kissing down her neck and across her chest. She groaned softly and threw back her head, letting her dark hair snake down her back. I licked her full left breast, instinct guiding me, and I was rewarded with a soft moan that escaped her lips. Emboldened, I took her dark pink nipple in my mouth and sucked it until it hardened, amazed at its satin-smooth feel. Gently, I bit it and tugged sharply, making her gasp. I moved on to her right breast, my erection throbbing with longing and her skin quivering under my touch.

As I continued, slowly sucking, tugging and biting, Jordan melted into my arms, whimpering with pleasure. Suddenly it seemed she couldn't take any more and she yanked down my pants and pulled me on to the couch.

I ran my hands up her calves and watched her writhe as I tickled the smooth, golden skin. Slowly, I edged my palms up her muscular thighs, stroking between her legs. She groaned and then gasped as I dipped my finger into her, rubbing gently. With fervent, grasping hands, she pulled off my underwear and took hold of my erection, tugging it. As my fingers moved faster and faster inside her, her hands moved faster and faster on me until my teeth were clenched and there was a tight, coiled heat in my groin that begged to be released.

I pushed her back and spread her legs apart. She smiled at me and entwined her arms around my neck, jerking me closer. I slammed into her, seeing her convulse and feeling a shock of my own pleasure shoot through my body at the warm wetness of hers. I began panting heavily and my mind numbed to the delicious satisfaction of pounding my hips. I moved slowly at first, relishing the new, exquisite sensation of being inside her, but then, as the excitement and pleasure began to increase, I thrust harder and deeper, pinning her against the couch.

We both groaned and moaned, our bodies heaving with each thrust. The heat in my groin began to overwhelm me and I closed my eyes and thrust harder and harder, pushing myself deeper and deeper inside her. Jordan grasped my shoulders and ran her hands across my chest and over my back, biting her nails into my skin with each moan of satisfaction. The pressure inside me increased to overflowing, leaving my head dizzy and hot until I could think of nothing else but Jordan lying beneath me in ecstasy. I pushed harder and faster and harder and faster and then suddenly I burst in an explosive high of adrenalin before collapsing in sweet relief.

We lay panting for a beautiful moment, our bodies sticky with dewy sweat. Jordan ran her fingernails lightly up and down my spine before tapping my shoulder and I moved off her . As I tried to regain composure, I watched Jordan arise from the couch cat-like, stretching her arms above her head and showing off the glorious silhouette of her full breasts resting against her slight ribcage. I stared mesmerised as she tugged the liquid silk dress back on and tidied her hair.

I was about to ask her what we should do now when she turned and abruptly left the room. I stared after her, stunned into silence and wishing that there was something I could say to bring her back.

Chapter Seven

When I emerged from the room some minutes later, I was shocked to discover guests fluttering about the mansion. They were clothed now and drinking and laughing as if nothing unusual had happened. It took me longer to relax. I wandered around rather ill at ease among swirls and eddies of people I didn't know. I was immediately struck by the number of young Englishmen dotted about; all well dressed, all looking a little hungry, and all talking in low, earnest voices to solid and prosperous Americans. I was sure that they were selling something: bonds or insurance or automobiles. They were at least agonisingly aware of the easy money in the vicinity and convinced that it was theirs for a few words in the right key. I wondered how on earth they could talk seriously to men whose wives they had been caressing only moments before.

I made an attempt to find my host, since I had little else to do, but the two or three people of whom I asked his whereabouts stared at me in such an amazed way, and denied so vehemently any knowledge of his movements, that I slunk off in the direction of the cocktail table – the only place in the garden where a single man could linger without looking purposeless and alone.

I was on my way to getting roaring drunk from sheer embarrassment when Jordan Baker reappeared at the edge of a group.

'Jordan!' I bellowed, advancing towards her. My voice seemed unnaturally loud across the garden.

'I wondered where you had gotten to,' she said as if it was I who had walked out after our sweet rapture and not her.

I was somewhat upset and confused, but she held my hand impersonally, as a promise that she'd take care of me in a minute, and gave ear to two girls in twin yellow dresses, who stopped at the foot of the steps.

'Hello!' they cried together. 'Sorry you didn't win.'

That was for the golf tournament. She had lost in the finals the week before – I had hungrily foraged as much information about Jordan Baker as I could since our last meeting.

'You don't know who we are,' said one of the girls in yellow, 'but we met you here about a month ago.'

'You've dyed your hair since then,' remarked Jordan, and I started, but the girls had moved casually on and her remark was addressed to the premature moon produced, like the supper no doubt, out of a caterer's basket.

With Jordan's slender golden arm resting in mine, we sauntered about the garden. A tray of cocktails floated at us through the twilight, and we sat down at a table with the two girls in yellow and three men, each one introduced to us as Mr Mumble.

'Do you come to these parties often?' enquired Jordan of the girl beside her.

'The last one was the one I met you at,' answered the girl, in an alert, confident voice. She turned to her companion: 'Wasn't it for you, Lucille?'

It was for Lucille, too.

'I like to come,' Lucille said. 'I never care what I do, so I always have a good time. When I was here last I tore my gown on a chair, and he asked me my name and address – inside of a week I got a package from Croirier's with a new evening gown in it.'

'Did you keep it?' asked Jordan.

'Sure I did. I was going to wear it tonight, but it was too

big in the bust and had to be altered. It was gas blue with lavender beads. Two hundred and sixty-five dollars.'

'There's something funny about a fellow that'll do a thing like that,' said the other girl eagerly. 'He doesn't want any trouble with anybody.'

'Who doesn't?' I enquired.

'Gatsby. Somebody told me that they—'

The two girls and Jordan leaned together confidentially.

'Somebody told me they thought he killed a man once.'

A thrill passed over all of us. The three Mr Mumbles bent forwards and listened eagerly.

'I don't think it's so much that,' argued Lucille sceptically; 'it's more that he was a German spy during the war.'

One of the men nodded in confirmation.

'I heard that from a man who knew all about him, grew up with him in Germany,' he assured us positively.

'Oh, no,' said the first girl, 'it couldn't be that, because he was in the American army during the war.' As our credulity switched back to her she leaned forwards with enthusiasm. 'You look at him sometimes when he thinks nobody's looking at him. I'll bet he killed a man.'

She narrowed her eyes and shivered. Lucille shivered. We all turned and looked around for Gatsby. It was testimony to the romantic speculation he inspired that there were whispers about him from those who found little that it was necessary to whisper about in this world.

The first supper – there would be another one after midnight – was now being served, and Jordan invited me to join her own party, who were spread around a table on the other side of the garden. There were three married couples and, much to my horror, Jordan's escort. I almost spluttered my drink when she introduced him. Jealously sprang up before I had even heard his name and I hated him instantly. He was a persistent undergraduate given to violent innuendo, and obviously under the impression that sooner or later Jordan was going to yield him up her person to a greater or lesser degree. He had floppy brown hair and limp hands. I knew his type from Yale all too well. I glared at him throughout the evening, endeavouring to get rid of him as soon as possible and fighting the thought that Jordan might well have already yielded to him and possibly enjoyed his passions more than mine. It made me feel violently sick.

'Let's get out,' whispered Jordan, after a somehow wasteful and inappropriate half-hour. 'This is much too polite for me.'

We got up, and she explained that we were going to find

the host: I had never met him, she said, and it was making me uneasy. The undergraduate nodded in a cynical, melancholy way and I cocked my head at him triumphantly.

The bar, where we glanced first, was crowded, but Gatsby was not there. She couldn't find him from the top of the steps, and he wasn't on the veranda. On a chance we tried an important-looking door, and walked into a high Gothic library, panelled with carved English oak, and probably transported complete from some ruin overseas.

A stout, middle-aged man, with enormous owl-eyed spectacles, was sitting somewhat drunk on the edge of a great table, staring with unsteady concentration at the shelves of books. As we entered he wheeled excitedly around and examined Jordan from head to foot.

'What do you think?' he demanded impetuously.

'About what?'

He waved his hand towards the bookshelves.

'About that. As a matter of fact you needn't bother to ascertain. I ascertained. They're real.'

'The books?'

He nodded.

'Absolutely real – have pages and everything. I thought they'd be a nice durable cardboard. Matter of fact, they're absolutely real. Pages and – Here! Lemme show you.'

Taking our scepticism for granted, he rushed to the bookcases and returned with Volume One of the *Stoddard Lectures.*

'See!' he cried triumphantly. 'It's a bona-fide piece of printed matter. It fooled me. This fella's a regular Belasco. It's a triumph. What thoroughness! What realism! Knew when to stop, too – didn't cut the pages. But what do you want? What do you expect?'

He snatched the book from me and replaced it hastily on its shelf, muttering that if one brick was removed the whole library was liable to collapse.

'Who brought you?' he demanded. 'Or did you just come? I was brought. Most people were brought.'

Jordan looked at him alertly, cheerfully, without answering.

'I was brought by a woman named Roosevelt,' he continued. 'Mrs Claud Roosevelt. Do you know her? I met her somewhere last night. I've been drunk for about a week now, and I thought it might sober me up to sit in a library.'

'Has it?'

'A little bit, I think. I can't tell yet. I've only been here an hour. Did I tell you about the books? They're real. They're—'

'You told us.'

We shook hands with him gravely and went back out-doors.

There was dancing now on the canvas in the garden; old men pushing young girls backwards in eternal graceless cir-cles, superior couples holding each other tortuously, fashionably, and keeping in the corners – and a great number of single girls dancing individualistically or reliev-ing the orchestra for a moment of the burden of the banjo or the traps. I had almost forgotten by now that hours before these same people had been thrusting and moaning at one another.

By midnight the hilarity had increased. A celebrated tenor had sung in Italian, and a notorious contralto had sung in jazz, and between the numbers people were doing 'stunts' all over the garden, while happy, vacuous bursts of laughter rose towards the summer sky. A pair of stage twins, who turned out to be the girls in yellow, did a baby act in costume, and champagne was served in glasses bigger than finger bowls. The moon had risen higher, and floating in the Sound was a triangle of silver scales, trembling a little to the stiff, tinny drip of the banjos on the lawn.

I was still with Jordan Baker. We were sitting at a table with a man of about my age and a rowdy little girl, who gave way upon the slightest provocation to uncontrollable laughter. I was enjoying myself now. I had taken two finger bowls of champagne, and the scene had changed before my eyes into something significant, elemental, and profound.

At a lull in the entertainment the man looked at me and smiled.

'Your face is familiar,' he said, politely. 'Weren't you in the Third Division during the war?'

'Why, yes. I was in the Ninth Machine-gun Battalion.'

'I was in the Seventh Infantry until June 1918. I knew I'd seen you somewhere before.'

We talked for a moment about some wet, grey little villages in France. Evidently he lived in this vicinity, for he told me that he had just bought a hydroplane, and was going to try it out in the morning.

'Want to go with me, old sport? Just near the shore along the Sound.'

'What time?'

'Any time that suits you best.'

It was on the tip of my tongue to ask his name when Jordan looked around and smiled.

'Having a good time now?' she enquired.

'Much better.' I turned again to my new acquaintance. 'This is an unusual party for me. I haven't even seen the host. I live over there –' I waved my hand at the invisible hedge in the distance, 'and this man Gatsby sent over his chauffeur with an invitation.' For a moment he looked at me as if he failed to understand.

'I'm Gatsby,' he said suddenly.

'What!' I exclaimed. 'Oh, I beg your pardon.'

'I thought you knew, old sport. I'm afraid I'm not a very good host.'

He smiled understandingly – much more than understandingly. It was one of those rare smiles with a quality of eternal reassurance in it that you may come across four or five times in life. It faced – or seemed to face – the whole external world for an instant, and then concentrated on you with an irresistible prejudice in your favour. It understood you just so far as you wanted to be understood, believed in you as you would like to believe in yourself, and assured you that it had precisely the impression of you that, at your best, you hoped to convey. Precisely at that point it vanished – and I was looking at an elegant young roughneck, a year or two over thirty, whose elaborate formality of speech just missed being absurd. Some time before he introduced himself I had got a strong impression that he was picking his words with care.

Almost at the moment when Mr Gatsby identified himself, a butler hurried towards him with the information that

Chicago was calling him on the wire. He excused himself with a small bow that included each of us in turn.

'If you want anything just ask for it, old sport,' he urged me. 'Excuse me. I will rejoin you later.'

When he was gone I turned immediately to Jordan — constrained to assure her of my surprise. I had expected that Mr Gatsby would be a florid and corpulent person in his middle years.

'Who is he?' I demanded. 'Do you know?'

'He's just a man named Gatsby.'

'Where is he from, I mean? And what does he do?'

'Now you're started on the subject,' she answered with a wan smile. 'Well, he told me once he was an Oxford man.' A dim background started to take shape behind him, but at her next remark it faded away. 'However, I don't believe it.'

'Why not?'

'I don't know,' she insisted, 'I just don't think he went there.'

Something in her tone reminded me of the other girl's 'I think he killed a man,' and had the effect of stimulating my curiosity. I would have accepted without question the information that Gatsby sprang from the swamps of Louisiana or from the Lower East Side of New York. That was comprehensible. But young men didn't — at least in my provincial inexperience I believed they didn't – drift coolly out of nowhere and buy a palace on Long Island Sound.

'Anyhow, he gives large . . . fun parties,' said Jordan. 'And I like *large* parties. They're so intimate. At small parties there isn't any privacy.'

I gulped and she moved a little closer to me for just a moment, pressing her hip against my side. She smiled suddenly, like a happy child, and then moved away again. I found my fingers twitching slightly by my sides, aching to pull her back.

There was the boom of a bass drum, and the voice of the orchestra leader rang out suddenly above the echolalia of the garden.

'Ladies and gentlemen,' he cried. 'At the request of Mr Gatsby we are going to play for you Mr Vladimir Tostoff's latest work, which attracted so much attention at Carnegie Hall last May. If you read the papers, you know there was a big sensation.' He smiled with jovial condescension, and added: 'Some sensation!' Whereupon everybody laughed. 'The piece is known,' he concluded lustily, 'as Vladimir Tostoff's "Jazz History of the World".'

The nature of Mr Tostoff's composition eluded me, because just as it began my eyes fell on Gatsby, standing alone on the marble steps and looking from one group to another with approving eyes. His tanned skin was drawn attractively tight on his face and his short hair looked as though it were trimmed every day. I could see nothing sinister about him. I wondered if the fact that he was not drinking helped to set him off from his guests, for it seemed to me that he grew more correct as the fraternal hilarity increased. When the 'Jazz History of the World' was over, girls were putting their heads on men's shoulders in a puppyish, convivial way, girls were swooning backwards playfully into men's arms, even into groups, knowing that someone would arrest their falls – but no one swooned backwards on Gatsby, and no French bob touched Gatsby's shoulder, and no singing quartets were formed with Gatsby's head for one link.

'I beg your pardon.'

Gatsby's butler was suddenly standing beside us.

'Miss Baker?' he enquired. 'I beg your pardon, but Mr Gatsby would like to speak to you alone.'

'With me?' she exclaimed in surprise.

'Yes, madame.'

She got up slowly, raising her eyebrows at me in astonishment, and followed the butler towards the house. My jealously surged back with a vengeance and I suddenly hated the man that I had previously been watching with curiosity. I had seen away the undergraduate, but I doubted that I could fare so well against the infamous Gatsby. I curled my hands into fists. I was alone and it was almost two. For some time confused and intriguing sounds had issued from a long, many-windowed room which overhung the terrace. Unable to stop myself, I went inside, following Gatsby and Jordan.

The large room was full of people. One of the girls in yellow was playing the piano, and beside her stood a tall, red-haired young lady from a famous chorus, engaged in song. She had drunk a quantity of champagne, and during the course of her song she had decided, ineptly, that everything was very, very sad – she was not only singing, she was weeping too. Whenever there was a pause in the song she filled it with gasping, broken sobs, and then took up the lyric again in a quavering soprano. The tears coursed down her cheeks – not freely, however, for when they came into contact with her heavily beaded eyelashes they assumed an inky colour, and pursued the rest of their way in slow black rivulets. A humorous suggestion was made that she sing the notes on her face, whereupon she threw up her hands, sank into a chair, and went off into a deep vinous sleep.

'She had a fight with a man who says he's her husband,' explained a girl at my elbow.

I looked around. Most of the remaining women were now having fights with men said to be their husbands. Even Jordan's party, the quartet from East Egg, were rent asunder by dissension. One of the men was talking with curious intensity to a young actress, and his wife, after attempting to laugh at the situation in a dignified and indifferent way, broke down entirely and resorted to flank attacks – at intervals she appeared suddenly at his side like an angry diamond, and hissed: 'You promised!' into his ear.

The reluctance to go home was not confined to wayward men. The hall was at present occupied by two deplorably sober men and their highly indignant wives. The wives were sympathising with each other in slightly raised voices. I wondered at a married couple that could happily let each other cavort with others. It felt wrong to me.

'Whenever he sees I'm having a good time he wants to go home,' one wife was saying.

'Never heard anything so selfish in my life,' replied the other.

'We're always the first ones to leave.'

'So are we.'

'Well, we're almost the last tonight,' said one of the men sheepishly. 'The orchestra left half an hour ago.'

In spite of the wives' agreement that such malevolence was beyond credibility, the dispute ended in a short struggle, and both wives were lifted, kicking, into the night.

The library opened and Jordan Baker and Gatsby came out together. He was saying some last word to her, but the eagerness in his manner tightened abruptly into formality as several people approached him to say goodbye. My spirits dropped and nasty visions of what they had been doing in the library slipped uninvited into my mind. I battled inwardly with myself, my fists clenching and unclenching with building rage.

Jordan's party began calling impatiently to her from the porch. She said goodbye to Gatsby and told her party that she would be a minute, before turning to me. I hadn't thought that she'd seen me standing in a corner of the hall and my rage began to dissipate as she approached, her breasts bouncing beneath the black liquid silk and her lips slightly parted. Apparently unable to read my seething expression, she whispered, 'I've just heard the most amazing thing. How long were we in there?'

I was thrown by this, wondering and hoping that I had misread the situation. 'About an hour,' I replied.

'It was — simply amazing,' she repeated abstractedly.

'But I swore I wouldn't tell it and here I am tantalising you.' She yawned gracefully in my face, her sweet breath brushing against my cheeks: 'Please come and see me ... Phone book ... Under the name of Mrs Sigourney Howard ... My aunt ...' She was hurrying off as she talked – her hips sashaying in a tempting way as she melted into the guests.

I guess she had assumed that I was leaving and I supposed I better had. I suddenly felt tired and dreamy, no doubt because I had received a blunt invitation to see Jordan Baker again. I did not want to go running after her this time at the risk of appearing too eager and, added to that, I was rather ashamed that on my first appearance I had stayed so late. I joined the last of Gatsby's guests, who were clustered around him. I wanted to explain that I'd hunted for him early in the evening and to apologise for not having known him in the garden. I also wanted to add a silent apology for hating him outright only a few minutes ago, thinking that he and Jordan were doing something untoward.

'I'm sorry ...' I began.

'Don't mention it,' he enjoined me eagerly. 'Don't give it another thought, old sport.' The familiar expression held no more familiarity than the hand which reassuringly brushed my shoulder. 'And don't forget we're going up in the hydroplane tomorrow morning, at nine o'clock.'

Then the butler, behind his shoulder: 'Philadelphia wants you on the phone, sir.'

'All right, in a minute. Tell them I'll be right there ... goodnight.'

'Goodnight.'

'Goodnight.' He smiled – and suddenly there seemed to be a pleasant significance in having been among the last to go, as if he had desired it all the time. 'Goodnight, old sport ... goodnight.'

But as I walked down the steps I saw that the evening was not quite over. Fifty feet from the door a dozen headlights illuminated a bizarre and tumultuous scene. In the ditch beside the road, right side up, but violently shorn of one wheel, rested a new coupé which had left Gatsby's drive not two minutes before. The sharp jut of a wall accounted for the detachment of the wheel, which was now getting considerable attention from half a dozen curious chauffeurs. However, as they had left their cars blocking the road, a harsh, discordant din from those in the rear had been audible for some time, and added to the already violent confusion of the scene.

A man in a long duster had dismounted from the wreck and now stood in the middle of the road, looking from the car to the tyre and from the tyre to the observers in a pleasant, puzzled way.

'See!' he explained. 'It went in the ditch.'

The fact was infinitely astonishing to him, and I recognised first the unusual quality of wonder, and then the man – it was the late patron of Gatsby's library.

'How'd it happen?'

He shrugged his shoulders.

'I know nothing whatever about mechanics,' he said decisively.

'But how did it happen? Did you run into the wall?'

'Don't ask me,' said Owl Eyes, washing his hands of the whole matter. 'I know very little about driving – next to nothing. It happened, and that's all I know.'

'Well, if you're a poor driver you oughtn't to try driving at night.'

'But I wasn't even trying,' he explained indignantly, 'I wasn't even trying.'

An awed hush fell upon the bystanders.

'Do you want to commit suicide?'

'You're lucky it was just a wheel! A bad driver and not even trying!'

'You don't understand,' explained the criminal. 'I wasn't driving. There's another man in the car.'

The shock that followed this declaration found voice in a sustained 'Ah-h-h!' as the door of the coupé swung slowly open. The crowd – it was now a crowd – stepped back involuntarily, and when the door had opened wide there was a ghostly pause. Then, very gradually, part by part, a pale, dangling individual stepped out of the wreck, pawing tentatively at the ground with a large uncertain dancing shoe.

Blinded by the glare of the headlights and confused by the incessant groaning of the horns, the apparition stood swaying for a moment before he perceived the man in the duster.

'Wha's matter?' he enquired calmly. 'Did we run outa gas?'

'Look!'

Half a dozen fingers pointed at the amputated wheel – he stared at it for a moment, and then looked upwards as though he suspected that it had dropped from the sky.

'It came off,' someone explained.

He nodded.

'At first I din' notice we'd stopped.'

A pause. Then, taking a long breath and straightening his shoulders, he remarked in a determined voice:

'Wonder'ff tell me where there's a gas'line station?'

At least a dozen men, some of them little better off than

he was, explained to him that wheel and car were no longer joined by any physical bond.

'Back out,' he suggested after a moment. 'Put her in reverse.'

'But the wheel's off!'

He hesitated.

'No harm in trying,' he said.

A car sweeping off in the distance caught my attention. It juddered around the commotion, its headlights waving erratically as it dipped off the road to zoom past others. I saw a flash of a golden, beautiful face laughing into the night and a swish of dark silky hair before it was gone. Something inside me glowed at the thought of Jordan Baker; something new and unfamiliar.

The caterwauling horns had reached a crescendo and I turned away and cut across the lawn towards home. I glanced back once. A wafer of a moon was shining over Gatsby's house, making the night fine as before, and surviving the laughter and the sound of his still-glowing garden. A sudden emptiness seemed to flow now from the windows and the great doors, endowing with complete isolation the figure of the host, who stood on the porch, his hand up in a formal gesture of farewell.

Chapter Eight

Reading over what I have written so far, I see I have given the impression that the events of three nights several weeks apart were all that absorbed me. It was not so much the events themselves that absorbed me but my new-found obsession with seeking out pleasure. It haunted my mind night and day. I began to wonder if I was taking after the notorious rogue Carraway, who scandalised society all those years ago. Judging from what I had seen at Gatsby's party, it seemed it would take a lot more to scandalise society these days, but my constant thirst for sex unnerved me. I suppose I had suppressed it for too long and now it was wreaking revenge.

However let it not be thought that I did nothing else but dream of Jordan Baker. Although this was an incessant pastime I managed to occupy myself in other ways also. Most of the time I worked. In the early morning the sun threw my shadow westwards as I hurried down the white chasms of lower New York to the Probity Trust. I knew the other clerks and young bond-salesmen by their first names, and lunched with them in dark, crowded restaurants on little pig sausages and mashed potatoes and coffee.

I took dinner usually at the Yale Club – for some reason it was the gloomiest event of my day – and then I went upstairs to the library and studied investments and securities for a conscientious hour. There were generally a few rioters around, but they never came into the library, so it was a good place to work. After that, if the night was mellow, I strolled down Madison Avenue past the old Murray Hill Hotel, and over Thirty-third Street to the Pennsylvania Station.

I liked New York, the racy, adventurous feel of it at night, and the satisfaction that the constant flicker of men and women and machines gives to the restless eye. I liked to walk up Fifth Avenue and pick out romantic women from the crowd and imagine that in a few minutes I was going to enter into their lives, and no one would ever know or disapprove. Sometimes, in my mind, I followed them to their apartments on the corners of hidden streets, and they turned and smiled back at me before they faded through a door into warm darkness. Sometimes I followed them. At the enchanted metropolitan twilight I often felt a haunting loneliness, and felt it in others – poor young clerks who loitered in front of windows waiting until it was time for a solitary restaurant dinner – young clerks in the dusk, wasting the most poignant moments of night and life.

Again at eight o'clock, when the dark lanes of the Forties were five deep with throbbing taxicabs, bound for the theatre district, I felt a sinking in my heart. Forms leaned together in the taxis as they waited, and voices sang, and there was laughter from unheard jokes, and lighted cigarettes outlined unintelligible gestures inside. Imagining that I, too, was hurrying towards gaiety and sharing their intimate excitement, I wished them well.

For a while I lost sight of Jordan Baker and saw her only in my dreams. I tried to call on her as she had suggested in our last meeting, but she evaded me. It took me a while to realise that a relationship with Jordan Baker is on Jordan Baker's terms. It was a difficult decision but I finally stopped making an effort to call on her or hear about her or see her. I dreamed about her constantly: her pert breasts, soft lips and curved hips sent me to sleep each night and often woke me sweating and aching, but I knew that running after her would get me nowhere.

And then in midsummer she found me, just as I had lost hope. She was cold and formal when we met, but she was there before me, as beautiful as I remembered. Our past actions were not alluded to and she treated me like a brother or a friend. I became frustrated. But I was beginning to understand the workings of Jordan Baker and even as her friend I was flattered to go places with a beautiful golf champion whose name everyone knew.

I began examining her and trying to work her out. There are better things I could have done with my time, but at least if I was scrutinising Jordan Baker then I was not racked with overwhelming sexual urges that kept me awake half the night. Her bored haughty face that she turned to the world concealed something – most affectations conceal something eventually, even though they don't in the beginning – and one day I found what it was. When we were at a house party together up in Warwick, she left a borrowed car out in the rain with the top down, and then lied about it – and suddenly I remembered the story about her. At her first big golf tournament there was a row that nearly reached the newspapers – a suggestion that she had moved her ball from a bad lie in the semi-final round. The thing approached the proportions of a scandal – then died away. A caddy retracted his statement, and the only other witness admitted that he might have been mistaken. The incident and the name had remained together in my mind.

Jordan Baker instinctively avoided clever, shrewd men, and now I saw that this was because she felt safer on a plane where any divergence from a code would be thought impossible. She was incurably dishonest. She wasn't able to endure being at a disadvantage and, given this unwillingness, I suppose she had begun dealing in subterfuges when she was very young in order to keep that cool, insolent smile turned to the world and yet satisfy the demands of her body.

It made no difference to me. Dishonesty in a woman is a thing you never blame deeply – I was casually sorry, and then I forgot. It was on that same house party that we had a curious conversation about driving a car. It started because she passed so close to some workmen that our fender flicked a button on one man's coat.

'You're a rotten driver,' I protested. 'Either you ought to be more careful, or you oughtn't to drive at all.'

'I am careful.'

'No, you're not.'

'Well, other people are,' she said lightly.

'What's that got to do with it?'

'They'll keep out of my way,' she insisted. 'It takes two to make an accident.'

'Suppose you met somebody just as careless as yourself.'

'I hope I never will,' she answered. 'I hate careless people. That's why I like you.'

Her grey, sun-strained eyes stared straight ahead, but she had deliberately shifted our relations, and for a moment I knew I loved her. I wanted her right then, in the car, but there were people around. She knew it too because she turned to me with a secret smile and flicked back her hair lightly.

'Can we go somewhere—' I began.

'Nick!' she scolded, still smiling, and her hand slid across the seat and travelled up my thigh, leaving a thrilling, tingling trail that made me gasp.

I glanced quickly out of the window, but everyone outside was absorbed with chatter and finding their motors. Jordan laughed at me and let her fingers creep a little further, closer to my crotch.

'You're not worried someone will see, are you?' she giggled.

I merely gasped as her fingers tickled my erection through the material of my pants and twirled her nail around the tip.

'Can we go somewhere—' I began again.

'We cannot!'

She laughed a deep, throaty laugh and I slumped back in my seat, knowing that she was toying with me, but unable to resist.

'Soon,' she whispered even though it was only she and I in the car. '*Soon*.'

I gulped, and she swung the car at a dangerous angle, past another parked motor, but this time I said nothing.

A relationship with Jordan Baker is on Jordan Baker's terms. I could never forget it.

Chapter Nine

O n Sunday morning while church bells rang in the villages alongshore, the world and its mistress returned to Gatsby's house and twinkled hilariously on his lawn. I was invited, but I came late. I was not ready to be part of that writhing mass yet. I had not given up hope on Jordan and, like some fanciful youth, I was saving myself for her. All other encounters paled in comparison. At one point, when I feared I had lost her and in the height of my erotic frenzy, I drove to a known brothel and sat outside in my motor. I stayed there a long time, fighting my thirst and telling myself that it would not be the same – this would not quench it. I finally came to my senses and drove home, but the idea that nothing else would do had stuck with me since. I remembered my antics with Catherine with disgust, thinking that I had sullied the imprint of

Jordan. I was aware that I was giving her too much prece-dence in my mind and my heart, but I was unable to stop myself.

At Gatsby's party, the second I had attended, I floated about looking for her, although she had already told me that she would not be there. I evidently did not believe her. Part of me was jealously looking, wondering if she had spent the morning bound and blindfolded like the rest of these guests, but another part of me just longed to see her. Despite it being a Sunday and despite it being the morning, I had heard groans and cries and gasps drifting across the clipped, emerald lawns on a light breeze that fluttered through my windows as I woke and that told me everything I needed to know. These people did not even need the cover of night to yield to their carnal cores. I was glad later as I wandered about that I did not see Jordan. Instead, I heard snippets of conversation and drank and ate as much as I could, unsure of what I had become.

'He's a bootlegger,' said the young ladies, moving some-where between his cocktails and his flowers. 'One time he killed a man who had found out that he was nephew to Von Hindenburg and second cousin to the devil. Reach me a rose, honey, and pour me a last drop into that there crystal glass.'

Once I wrote down on the empty spaces of a timetable the names of those who came to Gatsby's house that summer. It is an old timetable now, disintegrating at its folds, and headed 'This schedule in effect July 5th, 1922'. But I can still read the grey names, and they will give you a better impression than my generalities of those who accepted Gatsby's hospitality and paid him the subtle tribute of knowing nothing whatever about him.

From East Egg, then, came the Chester Beckers and the Leeches, and a man named Bunsen, whom I knew at Yale, and Dr Webster Civet, who was drowned last summer up in Maine. And the Hornbeams and the Willie Voltaires, and a whole clan named Blackbuck, who always gathered in a corner and flipped up their noses like goats at whosoever came near. And the Ismays and the Chrysties (or rather Hubert Auerbach and Mr Chrystie's wife), and Edgar Beaver, whose hair, they say, turned cotton-white one winter afternoon for no good reason at all.

Clarence Endive was from East Egg, as I remember. He came only once, in white knickerbockers, and had a fight with a bum named Etty in the garden. From farther out on the Island came the Cheadles and the O. R. P. Schraeders, and the Stonewall Jackson Abrams of Georgia, and the Fishguards and the Ripley Snells. Snell was there three days before he went to the penitentiary, so drunk out on the gravel drive that Mrs Ulysses Swett's automobile ran over his right hand. The Dancies came, too, and S. B. Whitebait, who was well over sixty, and Maurice A. Flink, and the Hammerheads, and Beluga the tobacco importer, and Beluga's girls.

From West Egg came the Poles and the Mulreadys and Cecil Roebuck and Cecil Schoen and Gulick the state senator and Newton Orchid, who controlled Films Par Excellence, and Eckhaust and Clyde Cohen and Don S. Schwartze (the son) and Arthur McCarty, all connected with the movies in one way or another. And the Catlips and the Bembergs and G. Earl Muldoon, brother to that Muldoon who afterwards strangled his wife. Da Fontano the promoter came there, and Ed Legros and James B. ('Rot-Gut') Ferret and the De Jongs and Ernest Lilly – they came to gamble, and when Ferret wandered into the garden it meant he was cleaned out and Associated Traction would have to fluctuate profitably next day.

A man named Klipspringer was there so often and so long that he became known as 'the boarder' – I doubt if he had any other home. Of theatrical people there were Gus

Waize and Horace O'Donavan and Lester Meyer and George Duckweed and Francis Bull. Also from New York were the Chromes and the Backhyssons and the Dennickers and Russel Betty and the Corrigans and the Kellehers and the Dewars and the Scullys and S. W. Belcher and the Smirkes and the young Quinns, divorced now, and Henry L. Palmetto, who killed himself by jumping in front of a subway train in Times Square.

Benny McClenahan arrived always with four girls. They were never quite the same ones in physical person, but they were so identical one with another that it inevitably seemed they had been there before. I have forgotten their names – Jacqueline, I think, or else Consuela, or Gloria or Jessie or Judy or June, and their last names were either the melodious names of flowers and months or the sterner ones of the great American capitalists whose cousins, if pressed, they would confess themselves to be.

In addition to all these I can remember that Faustina O'Brien came there at least once and the Baedeker girls and young Brewer, who had his nose shot off in the war, and Mr Albrucksburger and Miss Haag, his fiancée, and Ardita Fitz-Peters and Mr P. Jewett, once head of the American Legion, and Miss Claudia Hip, with a man reputed to be her chauffeur, and a prince of something, whom we called Duke, and whose name, if I ever knew it, I have forgotten.

All these people came to Gatsby's house in the summer.

At nine o'clock, one morning late in July, Gatsby's gorgeous car lurched up the rocky drive to my door and gave out a burst of melody from its three-noted horn. It was the first time he had called on me, though I had gone to two of his parties, mounted in his hydroplane, and, at his urgent invitation, made frequent use of his beach.

'Good morning, old sport. You're having lunch with me today and I thought we'd ride up together.'

He was balancing himself on the dashboard of his car with that resourcefulness of movement that is so peculiarly American — that comes, I suppose, with the absence of lifting work or rigid sitting in youth and, even more, with the formless grace of our nervous, sporadic games. This quality was continually breaking through his punctilious manner in the shape of restlessness. He was never quite still; there was always a tapping foot somewhere or the impatient opening and closing of a hand.

He saw me looking with admiration at his car.

'It's pretty, isn't it, old sport?' He jumped off to give me a better view. 'Haven't you ever seen it before?'

I'd seen it. Everybody had seen it. It was a rich cream colour, bright with nickel, swollen here and there in its monstrous length with triumphant hatboxes and supper-boxes and toolboxes, and terraced with a labyrinth of windshields that mirrored a dozen suns. Sitting down behind many layers of glass in a sort of green leather conservatory, we started to town.

I had talked with him perhaps half a dozen times in the past month and found, to my disappointment, that he had little to say. So my first impression, that he was a person of some undefined consequence, had gradually faded and he had become simply the proprietor of an elaborate roadhouse next door that held raucous, erotic gatherings. That part still interested me at least. I did wonder at a man that could so casually house such a thing, as if it were nothing.

I had the distinct feeling that he didn't ... partake in these orgies either. No one had told me so and Gatsby had said nothing that hinted at this, but I suppose I realised when I saw him for the first time, standing with his hands in his pockets, looking at the green light on the other side of the lake. The filthy gathering had been going on behind him, in his mansion, yet he was standing there, yearning for something else. Something across the lake.

It was a fancy of mine and not a fact, yet I still believed it. I wanted to ask Gatsby outright, but I knew I could not. Perhaps he would reveal something to me today. I wished to know so much more about him than I did.

And then came that disconcerting ride. We hadn't reached West Egg village before Gatsby began leaving his elegant sentences unfinished and slapping himself indecisively on the knee of his caramel-coloured suit.

'Look here, old sport,' he broke out surprisingly. 'What's your opinion of me, anyhow?'

A little overwhelmed, I began the generalised evasions which that question deserves.

'Well, I'm going to tell you something about my life,' he interrupted. 'I don't want you to get a wrong idea of me from all these stories you hear.'

So he was aware of the bizarre accusations that flavoured conversation in his halls.

'I'll tell you God's truth.' His right hand suddenly ordered divine retribution to stand by. 'I am the son of some wealthy people in the Middle West – all dead now. I was brought up in America but educated at Oxford, because all my ancestors have been educated there for many years. It is a family tradition.'

He looked at me sideways – and I knew why Jordan

Baker had believed he was lying. He hurried the phrase 'educated at Oxford' or swallowed it, or choked on it, as though it had bothered him before. And with this doubt, his whole statement fell to pieces, and I wondered if there wasn't something a little sinister about him, after all.

'What part of the Middle West?' I enquired casually.

'San Francisco.'

'I see.'

'My family all died and I came into a good deal of money.'

His voice was solemn, as if the memory of that sudden extinction of a clan still haunted him. For a moment I suspected that he was pulling my leg, but a glance at him convinced me otherwise.

'After that I lived like a young rajah in all the capitals of Europe – Paris, Venice, Rome – collecting jewels, chiefly rubies, hunting big game, painting a little, things for myself only, and trying to forget something very sad that had happened to me long ago.'

With an effort I managed to restrain my incredulous laughter. The very phrases were worn so threadbare that they evoked no image except that of a turbaned 'character' leaking sawdust at every pore as he pursued a tiger through the Bois de Boulogne.

'Then came the war, old sport. It was a great relief, and I tried very hard to die, but I seemed to bear an enchanted life. I accepted a commission as first lieutenant when it began. In the Argonne Forest I took two machine-gun detachments so far forward that there was a half-mile gap on either side of us where the infantry couldn't advance. We stayed there two days and two nights, a hundred and thirty men with sixteen Lewis guns, and when the infantry came up at last they found the insignia of three German divisions among the piles of dead. I was promoted to be a major, and every Allied government gave me a decoration – even Montenegro, little Montenegro down on the Adriatic Sea!'

Little Montenegro! He lifted up the words and nodded at them – with his smile. The smile comprehended Montenegro's troubled history and sympathised with the brave struggles of the Montenegrin people. It appreciated fully the chain of national circumstances which had elicited this tribute from Montenegro's warm little heart. My incredulity was submerged in fascination now; it was like skimming hastily through a dozen magazines.

He reached in his pocket, and a piece of metal, slung on a ribbon, fell into my palm.

'That's the one from Montenegro.'

To my astonishment, the thing had an authentic look.

'Orderi di Danilo,' ran the circular legend, 'Montenegro, Nicolas Rex.'

'Turn it.'

'"Major Jay Gatsby," I read, "For Valour Extraordinary".'

'Here's another thing I always carry. A souvenir of Oxford days. It was taken in Trinity Quad – the man on my left is now the Earl of Dorcaster.'

It was a photograph of half a dozen young men in blazers loafing in an archway through which were visible a host of spires. There was Gatsby, looking a little, not much, younger – with a cricket bat in his hand.

Then it was all true. I saw the skins of tigers flaming in his palace on the Grand Canal; I saw him opening a chest of rubies to ease, with their crimson-lighted depths, the gnawings of his broken heart.

'I'm going to make a big request of you today,' he said, pocketing his souvenirs with satisfaction, 'so I thought you ought to know something about me. I didn't want you to think I was just some nobody. You see, I usually find myself among strangers because I drift here and there trying to forget the sad thing that happened to me.' He hesitated. 'You'll hear about it this afternoon.'

'At lunch?'

'No, this afternoon. I happened to find out that you're taking Miss Baker to tea.'

'Do you mean you're in love with Miss Baker?'

'No, old sport, I'm not. But Miss Baker has kindly consented to speak to you about this matter.'

I hadn't the faintest idea what 'this matter' was, but I was more annoyed than interested. I hadn't asked Jordan to tea in order to discuss Mr Jay Gatsby. I was sure the request would be something utterly fantastic, and for a moment I was sorry I'd ever set foot upon his overpopulated lawn. A surge of jealousy had also welled within me; I did not appear to care that he had denied being in love with Jordan, I was still suspicious.

But he would not say another word. His correctness grew on him as we neared the city. We passed Port Roosevelt, where there was a glimpse of red-belted ocean-going ships, and sped along a cobbled slum lined with the dark, undeserted saloons of the faded-gilt 1900s. Then the valley of ashes opened out on both sides of us, and I had a glimpse of Mrs Wilson straining at the garage pump with panting vitality as we went by.

With fenders spread like wings we scattered light through half Long Island City – only half, for as we twisted among the pillars of the elevated I heard the familiar 'jug –

jug – spat!' of a motorcycle, and a frantic policeman rode alongside.

'All right, old sport,' called Gatsby. We slowed down. Taking a white card from his wallet, he waved it before the man's eyes.

'Right you are,' agreed the policeman, tipping his cap. 'Know you next time, Mr Gatsby. Excuse me!'

'What was that?' I enquired. 'The picture of Oxford?'

'I was able to do the commissioner a favour once, and he sends me a Christmas card every year.'

Over the great bridge, with the sunlight through the girders making a constant flicker upon the moving cars, with the city rising up across the river in white heaps and sugar lumps all built with a wish out of non-olfactory money. The city seen from the Queensboro Bridge is always the city seen for the first time, in its first wild promise of all the mystery and the beauty in the world.

A dead man passed us in a hearse heaped with blooms, followed by two carriages with drawn blinds, and by more cheerful carriages for friends. The friends looked out at us with the tragic eyes and short upper lips of south-eastern Europe, and I was glad that the sight of Gatsby's splendid car was included in their sombre holiday. As we crossed Blackwell's Island a limousine passed us, driven by a white chauffeur, in which sat three modish negroes, two bucks and a girl. I laughed aloud as the yolks of their eyeballs rolled towards us in haughty rivalry.

Anything can happen now that we've slid over this bridge, I thought; anything at all . . .

Even Gatsby could happen, without any particular wonder.

'I'm taking you to a place I know, old sport. I think you'll like it.'

And we sped off.

Roaring noon. In a well-fanned Forty-second Street cellar I met Gatsby for lunch. It was dark and fashionable. Blinking away the brightness of the street outside, my eyes picked him out obscurely in the anteroom, talking to another man.

He stood and smiled at me as I approached.

'Mr Carraway, this is my friend Mr Wolfsheim.'

A small, flat-nosed Jew raised his large head and regarded me with two fine growths of hair which luxuriated in either nostril. After a moment I discovered his tiny eyes in the half-darkness.

'– So I took one look at him,' said Mr Wolfsheim, shaking my hand earnestly, 'and what do you think I did?'

'What?' I enquired politely.

But evidently he was not addressing me, for he dropped my hand and covered Gatsby with his expressive nose.

'I handed the money to Katspaugh and I said: "All right, Katspaugh, don't pay him a penny till he shuts his mouth." He shut it then and there.'

Gatsby took an arm of each of us and moved forwards into the restaurant, whereupon Mr Wolfsheim swallowed a new sentence he was starting and lapsed into a somnambulatory abstraction.

'Highballs?' asked the head waiter.

'This is a nice restaurant here,' said Mr Wolfsheim, looking at the Presbyterian nymphs on the ceiling. 'But I like across the street better!'

'Yes, highballs,' agreed Gatsby, and then to Mr Wolfsheim: 'It's too hot over there.'

'Hot and small – yes,' said Mr Wolfsheim, 'but full of memories.'

'What place is that?' I asked.

'The old Metropole.'

'The old Metropole,' brooded Mr Wolfsheim gloomily. 'Filled with faces dead and gone. Filled with friends gone now for ever. I can't forget so long as I live the night they shot Rosy Rosenthal there. It was six of us at the table, and

Rosy had eaten and drunk a lot all evening. When it was almost morning the waiter came up to him with a funny look and says somebody wants to speak to him outside. "All right," says Rosy, and begins to get up, and I pulled him down in his chair. "Let the bastards come in here if they want you, Rosy, but don't you, so help me, move outside this room." It was four o'clock in the morning then, and if we'd of raised the blinds we'd of seen daylight.'

'Did he go?' I asked innocently.

'Sure he went.' Mr Wolfsheim's nose flashed at me indignantly. 'He turned around in the door and says: "Don't let that waiter take away my coffee!" Then he went out on the sidewalk, and they shot him three times in his full belly and drove away.'

'Four of them were electrocuted,' I said, remembering.

'Five, with Becker.' His nostrils turned to me in an interested way. 'I understand you're looking for a business gonnegtion.'

The juxtaposition of these two remarks was startling. Gatsby answered for me:

'Oh, no,' he exclaimed, 'this isn't the man.'

'No?' Mr Wolfsheim seemed disappointed.

'This is just a friend. I told you we'd talk about that some other time.'

'I beg your pardon,' said Mr Wolfsheim, 'I had the wrong man.'

A succulent hash arrived, and Mr Wolfsheim, forgetting the more sentimental atmosphere of the old Metropole, began to eat with ferocious delicacy. His eyes, meanwhile, roved very slowly all around the room – he completed the arc by turning to inspect the people directly behind. I think that, except for my presence, he would have taken one short glance beneath our own table.

'Look here, old sport,' said Gatsby, leaning towards me, 'I'm afraid I made you a little angry this morning in the car.'

There was the smile again, but this time I held out against it.

'I don't like mysteries,' I answered. 'And I don't understand why you won't come out frankly and tell me what you want. Why has it all got to come through Miss Baker?'

'Oh, it's nothing underhand,' he assured me. 'Miss Baker's a great sportswoman, you know, and she'd never do anything that wasn't all right.'

Suddenly he looked at his watch, jumped up, and hurried from the room, leaving me with Mr Wolfsheim at the table.

'He has to telephone,' said Mr Wolfsheim, following him

with his eyes. 'Fine fellow, isn't he? Handsome to look at and a perfect gentleman.'

'Yes.'

'He's an Oggsford man.'

'Oh!'

'He went to Oggsford College in England. You know Oggsford College?'

'I've heard of it.'

'It's one of the most famous colleges in the world.'

'Have you known Gatsby for a long time?' I enquired.

'Several years,' he answered in a gratified way. 'I made the pleasure of his acquaintance just after the war. But I knew I had discovered a man of fine breeding after I talked with him an hour. I said to myself: "There's the kind of man you'd like to take home and introduce to your mother and sister".' He paused. 'I see you're looking at my cuff buttons.'

I hadn't been looking at them, but I did now. They were composed of oddly familiar pieces of ivory.

'Finest specimens of human molars,' he informed me.

'Well!' I inspected them. 'That's a very interesting idea.'

'Yeah.' He flipped his sleeves up under his coat. 'Yeah, Gatsby's very careful about women. He would never so much as look at a friend's wife.'

I wondered if he knew about the erotic gatherings at the

Gatsby mansion. Surely he did? But I did not like to mention it now.

When the subject of this instinctive trust returned to the table and sat down Mr Wolfsheim drank his coffee with a jerk and got to his feet. He had apparently had enough.

'I have enjoyed my lunch,' he said, 'and I'm going to run off from you two young men before I outstay my welcome.'

'Don't hurry, Meyer,' said Gatsby, without enthusiasm.

Mr Wolfsheim raised his hand in a sort of benediction.

'You're very polite, but I belong to another generation,' he announced solemnly. 'You sit here and discuss your sports and your young ladies and your—' He supplied an imaginary noun with another wave of his hand. 'As for me, I am fifty years old, and I won't impose myself on you any longer.'

As he shook hands and turned away his tragic nose was trembling. I wondered if I had said anything to offend him.

'He becomes very sentimental sometimes,' explained Gatsby. 'This is one of his sentimental days. He's quite a character around New York – a denizen of Broadway.'

'Who is he, anyhow, an actor?'

'No.'

'A dentist?'

'Meyer Wolfsheim? No, he's a gambler.' Gatsby hesitated,

then added coolly: 'He's the man who fixed the World's Series back in 1919.'

'Fixed the World's Series?' I repeated.

The idea staggered me. I remembered, of course, that the World's Series had been fixed in 1919, but if I had thought of it at all I would have thought of it as a thing that merely happened, the end of some inevitable chain. It never occurred to me that one man could start to play with the faith of fifty million people – with the single-mindedness of a burglar blowing a safe.

'How did he happen to do that?' I asked after a minute.

'He just saw the opportunity.'

'Why isn't he in jail?'

'They can't get him, old sport. He's a smart man.'

I insisted on paying the check. As the waiter brought my change I caught sight of Tom Buchanan across the crowded room. His broad, solid frame was not easy to miss as it crouched in the squashed room.

'Come along with me for a minute,' I said; 'I've got to say hello to someone.'

When he saw us Tom jumped up and took half a dozen steps in our direction.

'Where've you been?' he demanded eagerly. 'Daisy's furious because you haven't called up.'

'This is Mr Gatsby, Mr Buchanan.'

They shook hands briefly, and a strained, unfamiliar look of embarrassment came over Gatsby's face that I didn't understand.

'How've you been, anyhow?' demanded Tom of me. Before I could form a reply he asked again, 'How'd you happen to come up this far to eat anyway?'

'I've been having lunch with Mr Gatsby.'

I turned towards Mr Gatsby, but he was no longer there.

Chapter Ten

That afternoon, I sat in the tea garden at the Plaza Hotel opposite Jordan Baker. She was sitting very straight on a straight chair, pushing a forkful of cake around her plate. Every so often she would pop a morsel in her mouth delicately and chew it slowly, licking her lips more than anybody ever need to. I had my legs crossed.

'Apparently you're to tell me something,' I said.

She was looking over my shoulder and I took the opportunity to glance at her breasts, which were straining against the confines of her thin blouse. There was a slight breeze blowing and I thought that I could make out the definition of her nipples. I shuddered.

'Cold?'

'Not at all.'

'And what am I supposed to be telling you?' she asked, treating me to the intense gaze of her deep, grey eyes.

'Something about Gatsby.'

So far our meeting had not been going as well as I had planned. She had been more dismissive of me than ever and silent too. Although I did not want Gatsby to intrude on our precious time together, at least if she was telling me this important thing then she was actually speaking. She appeared to be in a tight, pensive mood.

'Oh yes, that . . . ' she said, and she popped the last chunk of her cake in her mouth whole, biting on it hard.

I gulped.

'One October day in 1917 I was walking along from one place to another, half on the sidewalks and half on the lawns. I was happier on the lawns because I had on shoes from England with rubber knobs on the soles that bit into the soft ground. I had on a new plaid skirt also that blew a little in the wind, and whenever this happened the red, white, and blue banners in front of all the houses stretched out stiff and said tut-TUT-TUT-TUT, in a disapproving way.

'The largest of the banners and the largest of the lawns belonged to Daisy Fay's house. She was just eighteen, two years older than me, and by far the most popular of all the young girls in Louisville. She dressed in white, and had a little white roadster, and all day long the telephone rang in her house and excited young officers from Camp Taylor demanded the privilege of monopolising her that night.

'When I came opposite her house that morning her white roadster was beside the kerb, and she was sitting in it with a lieutenant I had never seen before. They were so engrossed in each other that she didn't see me until I was five feet away.

'"Hello, Jordan," she called unexpectedly. "Please come here."

'I was flattered that she wanted to speak to me, because of all the older girls I admired her most. She asked me if I was going to the Red Cross to make bandages. I was. Well, then, would I tell them that she couldn't come that day? The officer looked at Daisy while she was speaking in a way that every young girl wants to be looked at some time, and because it seemed romantic to me I have remembered the incident ever since. His name was Jay Gatsby, and I didn't lay eyes on him again for over four years – even after I'd met him on Long Island I didn't realise it was the same man.

'That was 1917. By the next year I had a few beaux myself, and I began to play in tournaments, so I didn't see

Daisy very often. She went with a slightly older crowd – when she went with anyone at all. Wild rumours were circulating about her – how her mother had found her packing her bag one winter night to go to New York and say goodbye to a soldier who was going overseas. She was effectually prevented, but she wasn't on speaking terms with her family for several weeks. After that she didn't play around with the soldiers any more, but only with a few flat-footed, short-sighted young men in town, who couldn't get into the army at all.

'By the next autumn she was gay again, gay as ever. She had a debut after the Armistice, and in February she was presumably engaged to a man from New Orleans. In June she married Tom Buchanan of Chicago, with more pomp and circumstance than Louisville ever knew before. He came down with a hundred people in four private cars, and hired a whole floor of the Seelbach Hotel, and the day before the wedding he gave her a string of pearls valued at three hundred and fifty thousand dollars.

'I was bridesmaid. I came into her room half an hour before the bridal dinner, and found her lying on her bed as lovely as the June night in her flowered dress – and as drunk as a monkey. She had a bottle of Sauternes in one hand and a letter in the other.

'"'Gratulate me," she muttered. "Never had a drink before, but oh how I do enjoy it."

'"What's the matter, Daisy?"

'I was scared, I can tell you; I'd never seen a girl like that before.

'"Here, deares'." She groped around in a waste-basket she had with her on the bed and pulled out the string of pearls. "Take 'em downstairs and give 'em back to whoever they belong to. Tell 'em all Daisy's change' her mind Say: "Daisy's change' her mind!"'

'She began to cry – she cried and cried. I rushed out and found her mother's maid, and we locked the door and got her into a cold bath. She wouldn't let go of the letter. She took it into the tub with her and squeezed it up into a wet ball, and only let me leave it in the soap-dish when she saw that it was coming to pieces like snow.

'But she didn't say another word. We gave her spirits of ammonia and put ice on her forehead and hooked her back into her dress, and half an hour later, when we walked out of the room, the pearls were around her neck and the incident was over. Next day at five o'clock she married Tom Buchanan without so much as a shiver, and started off on a three months' trip to the South Seas.

'I saw them in Santa Barbara when they came back, and

I thought I'd never seen a girl so mad about her husband. If he left the room for a minute she'd look around uneasily, and say: "Where's Tom gone?" and wear the most abstracted expression until she saw him coming in the door. She used to sit on the sand with his head in her lap by the hour, rubbing her fingers over his eyes and looking at him with unfathomable delight. It was touching to see them together – it made you laugh in a hushed, fascinated way. That was in August. A week after I left Santa Barbara Tom ran into a wagon on the Ventura road one night, and ripped a front wheel off his car. The girl who was with him got into the papers, too, because her arm was broken – she was one of the chambermaids in the Santa Barbara Hotel.

'The next April Daisy had her little girl, and they went to France for a year. I saw them one spring in Cannes, and later in Deauville, and then they came back to Chicago to settle down. Daisy was popular in Chicago, as you know. They moved with a fast crowd, all of them young and rich and wild, but she came out with an absolutely perfect reputation. Perhaps because she doesn't drink. It's a great advantage not to drink among hard-drinking people. You can hold your tongue, and, moreover, you can time any little irregularity of your own so that everybody else is so blind that they don't see or care. Perhaps Daisy never went in for amour at all – and yet there's something in that voice of hers . . .

'Well, about six weeks ago, she heard the name Gatsby for the first time in years. It was when I asked you – do you remember? – if you knew Gatsby in West Egg. After you had gone home she came into my room and woke me up, and said: "What Gatsby?" and when I described him – I was half asleep – she said in the strangest voice that it must be the man she used to know. It wasn't until then that I connected this Gatsby with the officer in her white car. The very same one.'

When Jordan Baker had finished telling all this we had left the Plaza for half an hour and were driving through Central Park. The sun had gone down behind the tall apartments of the movie stars in the West Fifties, and the clear voices of girls, already gathered like crickets on the grass, rose through the hot twilight:

'*I'm the Sheik of Araby, Your love belongs to me, At night when you're asleep, Into your tent I'll creep—*'

'It was a strange coincidence,' I said. 'A strange coincidence for Gatsby to be here at all and for Daisy too when she and Tom have been all over.'

'But it wasn't a coincidence at all.'

'Why not?'

'Gatsby bought that house so that Daisy would be just across the bay.'

He came alive to me, delivered suddenly from the womb of his purposeless splendour. I saw him standing, staring at the green light across the lake, uninterested in the erotic pleasures taking place behind him. He sought Daisy and nothing more. He hoped, perhaps, that she would hear those cries and gasps of pleasure and remember him.

'He wants to know,' continued Jordan, interrupting my thoughts, 'if you'll invite Daisy to your house some afternoon and then let him come over.'

The modesty of the demand shook me. He had waited five years and bought a mansion where he dispensed starlight to casual moths – so that he could 'come over' some afternoon to a stranger's garden.

'Did I have to know all this before he could ask such a little thing?'

'He's afraid, he's waited so long. He thought you might be offended. You see, he's a regular tough underneath it all.'

Something worried me.

'Why didn't he ask you to arrange a meeting?'

'He wants her to see his house,' she explained. 'And your house is right next door.'

'Oh!'

'I think he half expected her to wander into one of his parties, some night,' went on Jordan, 'but she never did. Then he began asking people casually if they knew her, and I was the first one he found. It was that night he sent for me at his dance, and you should have heard the elaborate way he worked up to it. Of course, I immediately suggested a luncheon in New York – and I thought he'd go mad: "I don't want to do anything out of the way!" he kept saying. "I want to see her right next door." When I said you were a particular friend of Tom's, he started to abandon the whole idea. He doesn't know very much about Tom, though he says he's read a Chicago paper for years just on the chance of catching a glimpse of Daisy's name.'

It was dark now, and as we dipped under a little bridge I put my arm around Jordan's golden shoulder and drew her towards me and asked her to dinner. Suddenly I wasn't thinking of Daisy and Gatsby any more, but of this clean, hard, limited person, who dealt in universal scepticism, and who leaned back seductively just within the circle of my arm.

'To dinner?' she enquired in her husky tone.

I would be lying if I said that I had not already thought of the alternative. Jordan had been keeping me at arm's length for so long and treating me like an older brother that I had scarcely thought the evening could turn into anything like that. Yet there was a small part of me that always hoped. I always hoped where she was concerned, knowing that hoping was all I ever could do. Her mood had changed considerably from earlier and I was almost thankful to Gatsby for giving us something to talk about.

'I thought you might be hungry,' I found myself whispering, almost waiting for her to laugh at me and drop her temptress stance.

'I am hungry, but not for food.'

'Really?'

'I'm starving.'

I glanced at her as we drove and her grey, cat-like eyes were flashing with desire in the soft moonlight. Her dark hair was swept back off her face by the wind blowing through the open window and it billowed behind her in a bruised cloud.

We were driving down a black, lonely street of tall, silent houses. I pulled over, bringing the motor to a smooth stop.

'You know someone living around here?' she asked.

I turned to her and shook my head.

'Then . . .' she trailed off as she caught the heat of my gaze.

Immediately she smiled widely and with slow deliberation, she moved her hand to her blouse and undid the first button.

'Do you think someone will see?' she whispered, shutting the window.

'I don't care,' I hissed back.

She giggled and pressed her lips against mine, guiding my hands across to her blouse so that I could continue undoing the buttons. I tore a few in my haste and felt her fingers groping for my belt buckle. I could scarcely believe that this was finally happening again, yet it seemed so natural.

As her soft lips gently worked over mine in rapid, delicate movements, I pulled her across the seats towards me and she began kissing my dark, stubbly chin and moving down my neck, leaving a trail of burning fire as she went – kissing, sucking and nipping with relish. I groaned and succumbed to her attack as she undid my shirt and ran her hands through the hair on my chest.

Quickly, with her mouth still firmly on mine, she hitched up her skirt and straddled me, leaning her back against the wheel and thrusting her hips into mine. I returned by pulling her blouse back and letting her bare breasts fall out into my cupped palms.

'Don't you have underwear?'

She giggled and kissed me hard. Then punished me by taking my bottom lip in her teeth and biting down.

My body began quivering with desire. She ran her hands down my front to my erection, which was stiff and throbbing under my pants, and she flicked it playfully with her fingers, smiling at me.

I shoved my hands under her skirt and moved them around to her large, curved behind. Taking each cheek in my hands, I stroked the smooth, firm skin and clutched and groped the tight muscles. She moaned softly into my mouth and undid my pants, diving beneath with her warm hands.

I gasped as she stroked and rubbed me. I moved my hands from her behind to between her legs and felt how wet she was. Her hips flexed into my hands as I teased her and I hitched her skirt up higher to plunge my fingers deep inside. She groaned and grasped my erection hard in response. As I gently hooked and rubbed my finger inside of her, she tugged me to the same rhythm until we were both panting and longing hungrily.

I could smell her sweet, fruity perfume mixed with the harsh scent of the leather seats. The street remained dark and silent outside, save for our gentle moaning and groaning. The thought that someone might at any point see us sent chilling thrills through my body that had me gasping all the harder.

Desperate for her, I pulled Jordan towards me, but she paused. Wordlessly, she reached behind her neck and unclasped a looped, gold chain.

'Give me your hands,' she said.

I frowned in confusion, but obeyed.

She put my wrists together and then wound the chain around them. I tried to pull away but she had it secured before I could.

'I want to lead,' she said by way of explanation, 'and you always try to take over.'

She jerked my hands back over her head and slapped her lips to mine with such force that it took my breath away. I tried to wind my hands into her hair, but couldn't. I was helpless as she began to trail more kisses across my neck and rake her nails down my back.

'See,' she whispered into my ear, before biting the lobe and thrusting her tongue inside, which sent shivers of delight coursing through me.

'Please,' I gasped.

She leaned back and looked at me with a wolfish grin. Taking my erection in one hand and rubbing it, she used the other to gently fondle my balls and lightly touch my thighs.

With her grey, sparkling eyes locked on mine, she tilted her hips forwards and gently pushed me inside her. I moaned with pleasure and rested my head against the seat, unable to touch her, or pull her down harder.

With a tantalisingly languid pace she rose and sank down, pulling me in and out of her. A hot, tight feeling began to coil in my stomach achingly slowly and I clenched my hands into fists above my head, longing to push her back against the wheel and pump in and out of her. But she continued at her leisurely pace, her stomach gently rippling with each thrust as I gritted my teeth.

Suddenly she raised herself higher and smashed quickly down on to me. I gasped as she began a new, fast pace, slamming into me with quick succession and groaning in my ear. Her breasts jiggled and I desperately wanted to grab them. I tried to move my wrists but the gold chain bit into my skin. I grimaced before the stab of pain mixed with the torrent of pleasure banking inside me and heightened it to a new extreme.

She cried out in pleasure, grabbing my shoulders in an orgasm, and I felt the burning desire inside me break forth as I came, bursting inside her with raw ecstasy.

She collapsed on to my chest and I rocked back against the leather seats, my head dizzy with pleasure. My pulse still beat through my body and my skin tingled. From the corner of my eye, I could see the windows of the motor were steamed up and I could not help but laugh.

'What is so funny?'

I didn't know how to reply so I gestured to my bound hands.

'Did you like it?' she purred.

'Is this something you learned in Gatsby's mansion?'

A shadow passed across Jordan's face and she regarded me coolly for a moment.

'I do believe you're small-minded, Nick Carraway.'

She said it lightly but I felt her jibe.

'It's just not me. It's not how I am.'

'I can tell.'

I couldn't believe that I was arguing with a beautiful woman who was straddling me with her breasts bare and lit in soft moonlight. I guess I had had enough of being pushed around by Jordan Baker. I was tired of being played a fool.

'Undo my hands.'

I didn't intend to sound so sharp and Jordan cocked a prettily arched brow at me, but she did as I said, and I thought she went about it with a little more respect than she usually allowed my way.

'Thank you,' I said, twisting my wrists about and rubbing the red skin.

She looped the chain back around her neck, watching me closely. The intense heat of her sun-stained eyes was something that I would never be able to ignore, despite my strong, self-assured words. She smiled at me playfully and leaned into my chest, her eyes locked on mine. And there it was – she saw it – my adoration that could not be hidden. Her smile widened and she licked her lips.

'Oh, Nick, we might make a Gatsby out of you one day.'

Chapter Eleven

When I came home to West Egg that night I was afraid for a moment that my house was on fire. Two o'clock and the whole corner of the peninsula was blazing with light, which fell unreal on the shrubbery and made thin elongating glints upon the roadside wires. Turning a corner, I saw that it was Gatsby's house, lit from tower to cellar.

At first I thought it was another party, a wild rout that had resolved itself into blindfolds and whips with all the house thrown open to the game. But there wasn't a sound. Only wind in the trees, which blew the wires and made the lights go off and on again as if the house had winked into the darkness. As my taxi groaned away I saw Gatsby walking towards me across his lawn.

'Your place looks like the World's Fair,' I said.

'Does it?' He turned his eyes towards it absently. 'I have

been glancing into some of the rooms. Let's go to Coney Island, old sport. In my car.'

'It's too late.'

'Well, suppose we take a plunge in the swimming pool? I haven't made use of it all summer.'

'I've got to go to bed.'

'All right.'

He waited, looking at me with suppressed eagerness.

'I talked with Miss Baker,' I said after a moment. 'I'm going to call up Daisy tomorrow and invite her over here to tea.'

'Oh, that's all right,' he said carelessly. 'I don't want to put you to any trouble.'

'What day would suit you?'

'What day would suit you?' he corrected me quickly. 'I don't want to put you to any trouble, you see.'

'How about the day after tomorrow?'

He considered for a moment. Then, with reluctance: 'I want to get the grass cut,' he said.

We both looked at the grass – there was a sharp line where my ragged lawn ended and the darker, well-kept expanse of his began. I suspected that he meant my grass.

'There's another little thing,' he said uncertainly, and hesitated.

'Would you rather put it off for a few days?' I asked.

'Oh, it isn't about that. At least—' He fumbled with a series of beginnings. 'Why, I thought – why, look here, old sport, you don't make much money, do you?'

'Not very much.'

This seemed to reassure him and he continued more confidently.

'I thought you didn't, if you'll pardon my – You see, I carry on a little business on the side, a sort of sideline, you understand. And I thought that if you don't make very much – You're selling bonds, aren't you, old sport?'

'Trying to.'

'Well, this would interest you. It wouldn't take up much of your time and you might pick up a nice bit of money. It happens to be a rather confidential sort of thing.'

I realise now that under different circumstances that conversation might have been one of the crises of my life. But, because the offer was obviously and tactlessly for a service to be rendered, I had no choice except to cut him off there.

'I've got my hands full,' I said. 'I'm much obliged but I couldn't take on any more work.'

'You wouldn't have to do any business with Wolfsheim.' Evidently he thought that I was shying away from the 'gonnegtion' mentioned at lunch, but I assured him he was wrong. He waited a moment longer, hoping I'd begin a conversation, but I was too absorbed to be responsive, so he went unwillingly home.

The evening had made me light-headed and happy; I think I walked into a deep sleep as I entered my front door and I was not woken in the night by wild arousal, the image of Jordan hot on my mind. So I didn't know whether or not Gatsby went to Coney Island, or for how many hours he 'glanced into rooms' while his house blazed gaudily on. I called up Daisy from the office next morning, and invited her to come to tea.

'Don't bring Tom,' I warned her.

'What?'

'Don't bring Tom.'

'Who is "Tom"?' she asked innocently.

The day agreed upon was pouring rain. At eleven o'clock a man in a raincoat, dragging a lawnmower, tapped at my front door and said that Mr Gatsby had sent him over to cut my grass. This reminded me that I had forgotten to tell my Finn to come back, so I drove into West Egg Village to search for her among soggy, whitewashed alleys and to buy some cups and lemons and flowers.

The flowers were unnecessary, for at two o'clock a greenhouse arrived from Gatsby's, with innumerable receptacles to contain it. An hour later the front door opened nervously, and Gatsby, in a white flannel suit, silver shirt, and gold-coloured tie, hurried in. He was pale, and there were dark signs of sleeplessness beneath his eyes.

'Is everything all right?' he asked immediately.

'The grass looks fine, if that's what you mean.'

'What grass?' he enquired blankly. 'Oh, the grass in the yard.' He looked out the window at it, but, judging from his expression, I don't believe he saw a thing.

'Looks very good,' he remarked vaguely. 'One of the papers said they thought the rain would stop about four. I think it was the *Journal.* Have you got everything you need in the shape of – of tea?'

I took him into the pantry, where he looked a little reproachfully at the Finn. Together we scrutinized the twelve lemon cakes from the delicatessen shop.

'Will they do?' I asked.

'Of course, of course! They're fine!' and he added hollowly, '. . . old sport.'

The rain cooled about half-past three to a damp mist, through which occasional thin drops swam like dew. Gatsby looked with vacant eyes through a copy of *Clay's Economics,* starting at the Finnish tread that shook the kitchen floor, and peering towards the bleared windows from time to time as if a series of invisible but alarming happenings were taking place outside. Finally he got up and informed me, in an uncertain voice, that he was going home.

'Why's that?'

'Nobody's coming to tea. It's too late!' He looked at his watch as if there was some pressing demand on his time elsewhere. 'I can't wait all day.'

'Don't be silly; it's just two minutes to four.'

He sat down miserably, as if I had pushed him, and simultaneously there was the sound of a motor turning into my lane. We both jumped up, and, a little harrowed myself, I went out into the yard.

Under the dripping bare lilac trees a large open car was coming up the drive. It stopped. Daisy's face, tipped sideways beneath a three-cornered lavender hat, looked out at me with a bright ecstatic smile.

'Is this absolutely where you live, my dearest one?'

The exhilarating ripple of her voice was a wild tonic in the rain. I had to follow the sound of it for a moment, up and down, with my ear alone, before any words came through. A damp streak of hair lay like a dash of blue paint across her cheek, and her hand was wet with glistening drops as I took it to help her from the car.

'Are you in love with me,' she said low in my ear, 'or why did I have to come alone?'

'That's the secret of Castle Rackrent. Tell your chauffeur to go far away and spend an hour.'

'Come back in an hour, Ferdie.' Then in a grave murmur: 'His name is Ferdie.'

'Does the gasoline affect his nose?'

'I don't think so,' she said innocently. 'Why?'

We went in. To my overwhelming surprise the living room was deserted.

'Well, that's funny,' I exclaimed.

'What's funny?'

She turned her head as there was a light dignified knocking at the front door. I went out and opened it. Gatsby, pale as death, with his hands plunged like weights in his coat pockets, was standing in a puddle of water glaring tragically into my eyes.

With his hands still in his coat pockets he stalked by me into the hall, turned sharply as if he were on a wire, and disappeared into the living room. It wasn't a bit funny. Aware of the loud beating of my own heart I pulled the door to against the increasing rain.

For half a minute there wasn't a sound. Then from the living room I heard a sort of choking murmur and part of a laugh, followed by Daisy's voice on a clear artificial note: 'I certainly am awfully glad to see you again.'

A pause; it endured horribly. I had nothing to do in the hall, so I went into the room.

Gatsby, his hands still in his pockets, was reclining against the mantelpiece in a strained counterfeit of perfect ease, even of boredom. His head leaned back so far that it rested against the face of a defunct mantelpiece clock, and from this position his distraught eyes stared down at Daisy, who was sitting, frightened but graceful, on the edge of a stiff chair.

'We've met before,' muttered Gatsby. His eyes glanced momentarily at me, and his lips parted with an abortive attempt at a laugh. Luckily the clock took this moment to tilt dangerously at the pressure of his head, whereupon he turned and caught it with trembling fingers, and set it back in place. Then he sat down, rigidly, his elbow on the arm of the sofa and his chin in his hand.

'I'm sorry about the clock,' he said.

My own face had now assumed a deep tropical burn. I couldn't muster up a single commonplace out of the thousand in my head.

'It's an old clock,' I told them idiotically.

I think we all believed for a moment that it had smashed in pieces on the floor.

'We haven't met for many years,' said Daisy, her voice as matter-of-fact as it could ever be.

'Five years next November.'

The automatic quality of Gatsby's answer set us all back at least another minute. I had them both on their feet with the desperate suggestion that they help me make tea in the kitchen when the demoniac Finn brought it in on a tray.

Amid the welcome confusion of cups and cakes a certain physical decency established itself. Gatsby got himself into a shadow and, while Daisy and I talked, looked conscientiously from one to the other of us with tense, unhappy eyes. However, as calmness wasn't an end in itself, I made an excuse at the first possible moment, and got to my feet.

'Where are you going?' demanded Gatsby in immediate alarm.

'I'll be back.'

'I've got to speak to you about something before you go.'

He followed me wildly into the kitchen, closed the door, and whispered:

'Oh, God!' in a miserable way.

'What's the matter?'

'This is a terrible mistake,' he said, shaking his head from side to side, 'a terrible, terrible mistake.'

'You're just embarrassed, that's all,' and luckily I added: 'Daisy's embarrassed too.'

'She's embarrassed?' he repeated incredulously.

'Just as much as you are.'

'Don't talk so loud.'

'You're acting like a little boy,' I broke out impatiently. 'Not only that, but you're rude. Daisy's sitting in there all alone.'

He raised his hand to stop my words, looked at me with unforgettable reproach, and, opening the door cautiously, went back into the other room.

I walked out the back way – just as Gatsby had when he had made his nervous circuit of the house half an hour before – and ran for a huge black knotted tree, whose massed leaves made a fabric against the rain. Once more it was pouring, and my irregular lawn, well shaved by Gatsby's gardener, abounded in small, muddy swamps and prehistoric marshes. There was nothing to look at from under the tree except Gatsby's enormous house, so I stared at it, like Kant at his church steeple, for half an hour. A brewer had built it early in the 'period' craze, a decade before, and there was a story that he'd agreed to pay five years' taxes on all the neighbouring cottages if the owners would have their roofs thatched with straw. Perhaps their refusal took the heart out of his plan to Found a Family – he went into an immediate decline. His children sold his house with the black wreath still on the door. Americans, while occasionally willing to be serfs, have always been obstinate about being peasantry.

After half an hour, the sun shone again, and the grocer's automobile rounded Gatsby's drive with the raw material for his servants' dinner – I felt sure he wouldn't eat a spoonful. A maid began opening the upper windows of his house, appeared momentarily in each, and, leaning from a large central bay, spat meditatively into the garden. It was time I went back. While the rain continued it had seemed like the murmur of their voices, rising and swelling a little now and then with gusts of emotion. But in the new silence I felt that silence had fallen within the house too.

I glanced over at it and started, shocked. Against the window-pane I could see two figures silhouetted, although they could easy be mistaken for one, entwined as they were. They appeared to be without the shadows of clothes and their hands clutched at, and clung to, each other desperately. I had to look away. It was not like the pleasure-seeking hunger I had witnessed in the manner and eyes of Gatsby's guests; it was altogether different. This was love and lust intermingled. The silhouettes grasped at each other like lost souls that had been parted for too long.

It was the way I felt about Jordan, but not the way she felt about me.

I stood under the tree a little while, no longer looking at anything in particular, but examining the inside of me. Seeing Daisy and Gatsby like that made me feel differently towards them. I had been irritated that I was forced to be their mediator – irritated that my love for Jordan could make me – but now I felt something new. I believe it was empathy.

I stood outside for as long as I could, but I eventually grew tired and cold. I reasoned that it would not do to let them go on for too long and so I went in – after making every possible noise in the kitchen, short of pushing over the stove – but I don't believe they heard a sound. I knocked for a long period on the door before entering and I heard giggles and scuffles from within before they called for me to enter.

They were sitting at either end of the couch, looking at each other as if some question had been asked, or was in the air, and every vestige of embarrassment was gone. Daisy's face was smeared with tears, and when I came in she jumped up and began wiping at it with her handkerchief before a mirror. But there was a change in Gatsby that was simply confounding. He literally glowed; without a word or a gesture of exultation a new well-being radiated from him and filled the little room.

'Oh, hello, old sport,' he said, as if he hadn't seen me for years. I thought for a moment he was going to shake hands.

'It's stopped raining.'

'Has it?' When he realised what I was talking about, that there were twinkle-bells of sunshine in the room, he smiled like a weatherman, like an ecstatic patron of recurrent light, and repeated the news to Daisy. 'What do you think of that? It's stopped raining.'

'I'm glad, Jay.' Her throat, full of aching, grieving beauty, told only of her unexpected joy.

'I want you and Daisy to come over to my house,' he said, 'I'd like to show her around.'

'You're sure you want me to come?'

'Absolutely, old sport.'

Daisy went upstairs to wash her face – too late I thought with humiliation of my towels – while Gatsby and I waited on the lawn.

'My house looks well, doesn't it?' he demanded. 'See how the whole front of it catches the light.'

I agreed that it was splendid.

'Yes.' His eyes went over it, every arched door and square

tower. 'It took me just three years to earn the money that bought it.'

'I thought you inherited your money.'

'I did, old sport,' he said automatically, 'but I lost most of it in the big panic – the panic of the war.'

I think he hardly knew what he was saying, for when I asked him what business he was in he answered, 'That's my affair,' before he realised that it wasn't the appropriate reply.

'Oh, I've been in several things,' he corrected himself. 'I was in the drug business and then I was in the oil business. But I'm not in either one now.' He looked at me with more attention. 'Do you mean you've been thinking over what I proposed the other night?'

Before I could answer, Daisy came out of the house and two rows of brass buttons on her dress gleamed in the sunlight.

'That huge place there?' she cried, pointing.

'Do you like it?'

'I love it, but I don't see how you live there all alone.'

'I keep it always full of interesting people, night and day. People who do interesting things. Celebrated people.'

Instead of taking the short cut along the Sound we went down the road and entered by the big postern. With enchanting murmurs Daisy admired this aspect or that of the feudal silhouette against the sky, admired the gardens, the sparkling odour of jonquils and the frothy odour of hawthorn and plum blossoms and the pale gold odour of kiss-me-at-the-gate. It was strange to reach the marble steps and find no stir of bright dresses in and out the door, and hear no sound but bird voices in the trees.

And inside, as we wandered through Marie Antoinette music-rooms and Restoration salons, I felt that there were guests concealed behind every couch and table, under orders to be breathlessly silent until we had passed through. There were certainly no whips or blindfolds to be seen. As Gatsby closed the door of the 'Merton College Library' I could have sworn I heard the owl-eyed man break into ghostly laughter.

We went upstairs, through period bedrooms swathed in rose and lavender silk and vivid with new flowers, through dressing-rooms and poolrooms, and bathrooms with sunken baths – intruding into one chamber where a dishevelled man in pyjamas was doing liver exercises on the floor. It was Mr Klipspringer, the 'boarder'. I had seen him wandering hungrily about the beach that morning. Finally we came to Gatsby's own apartment, a bedroom and a bath, and an Adam study, where we sat down and drank a glass of some Chartreuse he took from a cupboard in the wall.

He hadn't once ceased looking at Daisy, and I think he revalued everything in his house according to the measure of response it drew from her well-loved eyes. Sometimes, too, he stared around at his possessions in a dazed way, as though in her actual and astounding presence none of it was any longer real. Once he nearly toppled down a flight of stairs.

His bedroom was the simplest room of all – except where the dresser was garnished with a toilet set of pure dull gold. Daisy took the brush with delight, and smoothed her hair, whereupon Gatsby sat down and shaded his eyes and began to laugh.

'It's the funniest thing, old sport,' he said hilariously. 'I can't— When I try to—'

He had passed visibly through two states and was entering upon a third. After his embarrassment and his unreasoning joy he was consumed with wonder at her presence. He had been full of the idea so long, dreamed it right through to the end, waited with his teeth set, so to speak, at an inconceivable pitch of intensity. Now, in the reaction, he was running down like an overwound clock.

Recovering himself in a minute he opened for us two hulking patent cabinets which held his massed suits and dressing gowns and ties, and his shirts, piled like bricks in stacks a dozen high.

'I've got a man in England who buys me clothes. He sends over a selection of things at the beginning of each season, spring and fall.'

He took out a pile of shirts and began throwing them, one by one, before us, shirts of sheer linen and thick silk and fine flannel, which lost their folds as they fell and covered the table in many-coloured disarray. While we admired he brought more and the soft rich heap mounted higher – shirts with stripes and scrolls and plaids in coral and apple-green and lavender and faint orange, and monograms of Indian blue. Suddenly, with a strained sound, Daisy bent her head into the shirts and began to cry stormily.

'They're such beautiful shirts,' she sobbed, her voice muffled in the thick folds. 'It makes me sad because I've never seen such – such beautiful shirts before.'

After the house, we were to see the grounds and the swimming pool, and the hydroplane and the midsummer flowers – but outside Gatsby's window it began to rain again, so we stood in a row looking at the corrugated surface of the Sound.

'If it wasn't for the mist we could see your home across the bay,' said Gatsby. 'You always have a green light that burns all night at the end of your dock.'

Daisy put her arm through his abruptly, but he seemed absorbed in what he had just said. Possibly it had occurred to him that the colossal significance of that light had now vanished for ever. Compared to the great distance that had separated him from Daisy it had seemed very near to her, almost touching her. It had seemed as close as a star to the moon. Now it was again a green light on a dock. His count of enchanted objects had diminished by one.

I began to walk about the room, examining various indefinite objects in the half darkness. A large photograph of an elderly man in yachting costume attracted me, hung on the wall over his desk.

'Who's this?'

'That? That's Mr Dan Cody, old sport.'

The name sounded faintly familiar.

'He's dead now. He used to be my best friend years ago.'

There was a small picture of Gatsby, also in yachting costume, on the bureau – Gatsby with his head thrown back defiantly – taken apparently when he was about eighteen.

'I adore it,' exclaimed Daisy. 'The pompadour! You never told me you had a pompadour – or a yacht.'

'Look at this,' said Gatsby quickly. 'Here's a lot of clippings – about you.'

They stood side by side examining it. I was going to ask

to see the rubies when the phone rang, and Gatsby took up the receiver.

'Yes ... well, I can't talk now ... I can't talk now, old sport ... I said a small town ... he must know what a small town is ... well, he's no use to us if Detroit is his idea of a small town ... well, it's not a small town ... enough ... '

He rang off.

'Come here quick!' cried Daisy at the window.

The rain was still falling, but the darkness had parted in the west, and there was a pink and golden billow of foamy clouds above the sea.

'Look at that,' she whispered, and then after a moment: 'I'd like to just get one of those pink clouds and put you in it and push you around.'

I tried to go then, but they wouldn't hear of it; perhaps my presence made them feel more satisfactorily alone.

'I know what we'll do,' said Gatsby, 'we'll have Klip-springer play the piano.'

He went out of the room calling 'Ewing!' and returned in a few minutes accompanied by an embarrassed, slightly worn young man, with shell-rimmed glasses and scanty blond hair. He was now decently clothed in a 'sport shirt' open at the neck, sneakers, and duck pants of a nebulous hue.

'Did we interrupt your exercises?' enquired Daisy politely.

'I was asleep,' cried Mr Klipspringer, in a spasm of embarrassment. 'That is, I'd been asleep. Then I got up, but . . .'

'Klipspringer plays the piano,' said Gatsby, cutting him off. 'Don't you, Ewing, old sport?'

'I don't play well. I don't – I hardly play at all. I'm all out of prac—'

'We'll go downstairs,' interrupted Gatsby. He flipped a switch. The grey windows disappeared as the house glowed full of light.

In the music room Gatsby turned on a solitary lamp beside the piano. He lit Daisy's cigarette from a trembling match, and sat down with her on a couch far across the room, where there was no light save what the gleaming floor bounced in from the hall.

As Klipspringer began to play, I could not help but notice the two of them cavorting together like lovesick fools. Gatsby's hands roamed from Daisy's waist to her chest, touching and tickling her so that she giggled breathlessly. He curled his fingers around her hair, caressed her delicate hands, kissed her neck and blew into her ear. At one point, I thought I saw him sneak a hand up her dress, but I tried not to notice.

They had me thinking too keenly of Jordan. I was desperate to see her, but I knew that if I wanted our meeting to be anything like our last then I should wait and let her come to me on her own terms. Listening to their soft whispers, I saw Jordan's bare breasts in moonlight and felt her undulating on top of me, her toned stomach rippling with each thrust. My erection throbbed between my legs and I swallowed hard. I would be racked with dreams of her tonight.

When Klipspringer had played 'The Love Nest', he turned around on the bench and searched unhappily for Gatsby in the gloom.

'I'm all out of practice, you see. I told you I couldn't play. I'm all out of prac—'

'Don't talk so much, old sport,' commanded Gatsby. 'Play!'

"'In the morning, In the evening, Ain't we got fun—'"

Outside the wind was loud and there was a faint flow of thunder along the Sound. All the lights were going on in West Egg now; the electric trains, men-carrying, were plunging home through the rain from New York. It was the hour of a profound human change, and excitement was generating on the air.

"'One thing's sure and nothing's surer, The rich get richer

and the poor get— children. In the meantime, In between time—"'

As I went over to say goodbye I saw that the expression of bewilderment had come back into Gatsby's face, as though a faint doubt had occurred to him as to the quality of his present happiness. Almost five years! There must have been moments even that afternoon when Daisy tumbled short of his dreams – not through her own fault, but because of the colossal vitality of his illusion. It had gone beyond her, beyond everything. He had thrown himself into it with a creative passion, adding to it all the time, decking it out with every bright feather that drifted his way. No amount of fire or freshness can challenge what a man will store up in his ghostly heart.

As I watched him he adjusted himself a little, visibly. His hand took hold of hers, and as she said something low in his ear he turned towards her with a rush of emotion. I think that voice held him most, with its fluctuating, feverish warmth, because it couldn't be over-dreamed – that voice was a deathless song.

They had forgotten me, but Daisy glanced up and held out her hand; Gatsby didn't know me now at all. I looked once more at them and they looked back at me, remotely, possessed by intense life. Then I went out of the room and down the marble steps into the rain, leaving them there together.

That night I barely slept at all, instead I dreamed of cat-like eyes, curved hips and golden skin. I woke constantly in a filmy sweat, aching.

Chapter Twelve

I didn't see Jordan until some days later and, that morning, I was in a frenzy. I wondered feverishly what would become of this meeting. Rationale told me that I was simply taking her to dinner, but my thoughts roamed further. The memory of her legs straddling my waist in the moonlight as we sat in my motor came again and again to my mind. I fervently wanted this meeting to be the same and I played through several scenarios on the way to her aunt's house; each one more audacious and unrealistic than the last. It's a credit to my self-control that I didn't greet her with a throbbing erection, though I'm sure she wouldn't have minded.

But all hope vanished when I arrived to collect her. She opened the door as I walked on to the front step and caught me unawares. She was not dressed for going out; in fact, her loose blouse and wide-leg pants suggested quite the opposite.

'Yes?'

I blinked at her. Her expression was one of polite inter-est, as if we had just bumped into one another at a garden party.

'Dinner . . .' I trailed off.

I wondered if she was pretending that she'd forgotten our plans. She'd done this before and my heart sank at the thought. Having made such progress in our last meeting, I was afraid that we would fall once more into the frustrating cate-gory of 'friends'. I wasn't sure that my weakened emotions could handle another such battering.

Suddenly she grinned and I knew the grin. My hands shook a little.

'Nick, you are so easy,' she giggled.

'I am?'

She tugged on my arms and pulled me inside, glancing over my shoulder at the street as she shut the door.

'Do you think many people saw you?' she asked.

'Does that really matter? They'll see my car.'

'Yes, you're right. Let's hope they don't know that my aunt isn't here.'

I had followed her into a nice neat front room and I almost tripped over the leg of a couch.

'Not here?' I gulped.

She held my gaze and widened her grin slightly so that I could see every one of her straight white teeth.

'I thought that we could have some fun; you didn't particularly want to go to dinner, did you?'

I shook my head.

'Nick, you are so easy.'

I did not care. All I could think was that Jordan Baker was standing in front of me, her slim waist encased in tight pants that skimmed her pert backside and curved over her hips. I longed to touch her again, to feel her warm golden skin and silky dark hair. I wanted to be inside her.

'My aunt will be gone some time so we'll have the place to ourselves.' Her voice spun across the room as she went about drawing the curtains. 'We don't want anyone to see,' she added.

'In here?'

'Well why not?'

'I . . .'

'Oh, Nick.'

She stuck out her bottom lip and pouted at me through her lashes. Her cat-like eyes drew me in as she slowly unbuttoned the top of her blouse. She stopped just as she came to the tantalising dip of her cleavage and let her arms fall by her sides.

'Perhaps we should go for that wretched dinner after all—'

'No!'

I had not meant to cry out and I saw her eyes alight with pleasure at my malleable nature. She had me under her thumb and we both knew it. I silently cursed myself.

'No?'

I shook my head.

'Then what?'

Slowly, I let my jacket slide from my shoulders and fall to the floor.

Jordan giggled. 'See, Nick, it's not so bad . . .'

Without waiting for a reply, I ripped off my tie and began pulling at my shirt. Jordan looked a little startled at first and I relished her unease. I was tired of constantly being one step behind her.

With my chest bare, I strode across the room and pulled her to me. She gasped and clutched me in return, raising her lips to my own. They were as sweet and soft as I remembered them and I kissed her slowly at first, savouring the taste, before my passion overtook me and I became fervent and hard.

Yearning pumped through my whole body, filling me with desperate need. My erection was stiff and began pulsing, aching for her. I could feel her skin shivering under my touch with desire and it burned my palms, its golden hue blistering like caramel. Her hands stroked my chest, tugged the dark hair between my pecs and caressed the taut skin of my stomach.

I pulled away, both of us panting for breath. Her eyes scorched into mine, their intensity thrilling me and their expression begging. I was blinded by my own desire and suddenly the fact that we were in her aunt's front room did not matter. The drawn curtains created a shadowed dimness that bathed everything in soft grey light. I did not see the couches or the paintings; they were obscure outlines. All I saw was Jordan; her blazing eyes and the delectable contours of her body.

In one rapid movement I tore the buttons from her blouse and pulled it off her shoulders. It fluttered to the ground as I ran my hands across the smooth skin of her stomach. She sighed into my neck as I skimmed my palms up to her breasts, feeling their plump curves. In return, she ran her nails up and down my back, leaving scratches of pleasure that had me shuddering in delight.

Her hand snaked its way to my crotch and she fondled the bulge of my pants, meanwhile kissing the tender skin on my neck. Quickly she flicked the catch of my belt and pulled down my pants. I gasped into her dark, silky hair as she let her fingers leisurely roam from my navel downwards.

I shivered as she touched my erection, gently brushing its tip with her fingers. While she stroked it, she kissed me, flicking her tongue across my lips in time to her caresses. I felt a rush of pleasure and a jolt of heat shoot through my stomach.

'Again,' whispered Jordan in my ear, nipping my earlobe playfully.

It was only then that I realised that I had uttered her name. I did so again, rubbing my hands against her and watching her eyes glaze with longing. I began undoing her pants, fumbling in my haste and shaking as she continued to stroke me. I pulled them down and they pooled on the floor, next to her blouse.

Jordan paused and, without breaking my gaze, she slowly peeled off her underwear, watching my hunger for her magnify. She was as I remembered her and her golden curves looked even better somehow in the shadowed light. Without the faintest trace of unease at being completely naked, she fell back on to the nearest couch, reclining on it languidly.

She giggled at me and shrugged. She had control. I wanted to wipe the smug smile from her beautiful face so

I dropped on my knees in front of her and took hold of her ankles. She looked at me in surprise as I tugged them towards me, tilting her backwards.

'What—'

Her words were lost in a gasp of surprise as I buried my head between her legs and licked her. She was warm and hot and wet, and I hooked her legs over my shoulders. Breaking away, I kissed each of her muscular thighs, leaving a burning trail between her legs, which I returned to again, darting my tongue inside her.

She cried out and clutched at a pillow, her body bowing in pleasure. I continued to lick and kiss her, instinct guiding me and my own desire building further. She was panting and breathless and then groaning softly as I pushed my tongue further inside her, my hands caressing her hips.

Suddenly her body quivered and she called out my name before lying still.

I pulled away and kissed each of her knees.

'It's your turn,' she whispered between breaths.

I shook my head as I stood and her brow crumpled.

'What do you mean?'

'That was enough for me.'

You are enough for me, I added silently, but instead of saying it, I pulled on my shirt.

She watched me, confused.

'But . . .'

'How about that wretched dinner?'

She stood, her chest still heaving. She was staring at me with an expression that I'd never seen before.

'You must be hungry after that?' I added with a painful attempt at humour.

She regarded me silently for a moment and then she came and gently and sincerely kissed me on the cheek.

The next day I saw Jordan again. Nothing explicit happened; I only took her to supper that evening and then dropped her home to her aunt's house. But it was altogether more than that. Something in Jordan's manner had changed towards me. It was slight, but her treatment of me was . . . gentle. During supper I caught her looking at me often with a searching, grey gaze that was trying to figure me out. I was mightily tempted to come clean right then and there, telling her how I felt for her, but I was worried of frightening her away. I am glad I didn't, or else I don't think I would have received a second parting kiss: a sweet and smooth stain on my cheek, that lingered long after I had dropped her off and was driving home alone in the darkness.

However, something all the more interesting happened

that day. In the morning an ambitious young reporter from New York arrived at Gatsby's door out of the blue and asked him if he had anything to say.

'Anything to say about what?' enquired Gatsby politely.

'Why – any statement to give out.'

It transpired after a confused five minutes that the man had heard Gatsby's name around his office in a connection which he either wouldn't reveal or didn't fully understand. This was his day off and with laudable initiative he had hurried out 'to see'.

It was a random shot, and yet the reporter's instinct was right. Gatsby's notoriety, spread about by the hundreds who had accepted his hospitality and so become authorities on his past, had increased all summer until he fell just short of being news. Contemporary legends such as the 'underground pipeline to Canada' attached themselves to him, and there was one persistent story that he didn't live in a house at all, but in a boat that looked like a house and was moved secretly up and down the Long Island shore. Just why these inventions were a source of satisfaction to James Gatz of North Dakota, isn't easy to say.

James Gatz – that was really, or at least legally, his name. He had changed it at the age of seventeen and at the specific moment that witnessed the beginning of his career –

when he saw Dan Cody's yacht drop anchor over the most insidious flat on Lake Superior. It was James Gatz who had been loafing along the beach that afternoon in a torn green jersey and a pair of canvas pants, but it was already Jay Gatsby who borrowed a rowboat, pulled out to the *Tuolomee*, and informed Cody that a wind might catch him and break him up in half an hour.

I suppose he'd had the name ready for a long time, even then. His parents were shiftless and unsuccessful farm people – his imagination had never really accepted them as his parents at all. The truth was that Jay Gatsby of West Egg, Long Island, sprang from his Platonic conception of himself. He was a son of God – a phrase which, if it means anything, means just that – and he must be about His Father's business, the service of a vast, vulgar, and meretricious beauty. So he invented just the sort of Jay Gatsby that a seventeen-year-old boy would be likely to invent, and to this conception he was faithful to the end.

For over a year he had been beating his way along the south shore of Lake Superior as a clam-digger and a salmon-fisher or in any other capacity that brought him food and bed. His brown, hardening body lived naturally through the half-fierce, half-lazy work of the bracing days. He knew women early, and since they spoiled him he became contemptuous of them, of young virgins because they were ignorant, of the others because they were hysterical about things which in his overwhelming self-absorption he took for granted.

But his heart was in a constant, turbulent riot. The most grotesque and fantastic conceits haunted him in his bed at night. A universe of ineffable gaudiness spun itself out in his brain while the clock ticked on the washstand and the moon soaked with wet light his tangled clothes upon the floor. Each night he added to the pattern of his fancies until drowsiness closed down upon some vivid scene with an oblivious embrace. For a while these reveries provided an outlet for his imagination; they were a satisfactory hint of the unreality of reality, a promise that the rock of the world was founded securely on a fairy's wing.

An instinct towards his future glory had led him, some months before, to the small Lutheran college of St Olaf in southern Minnesota. He stayed there two weeks, dismayed at its ferocious indifference to the drums of his destiny, to destiny itself, and despising the janitor's work with which he was to pay his way through. Then he drifted back to Lake Superior, and he was still searching for something to do on the day that Dan Cody's yacht dropped anchor in the shallows alongshore.

Cody was fifty years old then, a product of the Nevada silver fields, of the Yukon, of every rush for metal since '75. The transactions in Montana copper that made him many times a millionaire found him physically robust but on the verge of soft-mindedness and, suspecting this, an infinite number of women tried to separate him from his money. The none-too-savoury ramifications by which Ella Kaye, the newspaper woman, played Madame de Maintenon to his weakness and sent him to sea in a yacht, were common knowledge to the turgid sub-journalism of 1902. He had been coasting along all-too-hospitable shores for five years when he turned up as James Gatz's destiny at Little Girls Point.

To the young Gatz, resting on his oars and looking up at the railed deck, the yacht represented all the beauty and glamour in the world. I suppose he smiled at Cody – he had probably discovered that people liked him when he smiled. At any rate Cody asked him a few questions (one of them elicited the brand-new name) and found that he was quick and extravagantly ambitious. A few days later he took him to Duluth and bought him a blue coat, six pair of white duck pants, and a yachting cap. And when the *Tuolomee* left for the West Indies and the Barbary Coast, Gatsby left too.

He was employed in a vague personal capacity – while he remained with Cody he was in turn steward, mate, skipper, secretary, and even jailer, for Dan Cody sober knew what lavish doings Dan Cody drunk might soon be about, and he provided for such contingencies by reposing more and more trust in Gatsby. The arrangement lasted five years, during which the boat went three times around the continent. It might have lasted indefinitely except for the fact that Ella Kaye came on board one night in Boston and a week later Dan Cody inhospitably died.

I remember the portrait of him up in Gatsby's bedroom, a grey, florid man with a hard, empty face – the pioneer debauchee, who during one phase of American life brought back to the Eastern seaboard the savage violence of }the frontier brothel and saloon. It was indirectly due to Cody that Gatsby drank so little. Sometimes in the course of gay parties women used to rub champagne into his hair; for himself he formed the habit of letting liquor alone.

And it was from Cody that he inherited money – a legacy of twenty-five thousand dollars. He didn't get it. He never understood the legal device that was used against him, but what remained of the millions went intact to Ella Kaye. He was left with his singularly appropriate education;

the vague contour of Jay Gatsby had filled out to the sub-stantiality of a man.

He told me all this very much later, but I've put it down here with the idea of exploding those first wild rumours about his antecedents, which weren't even faintly true. Moreover he told it to me at a time of confusion, when I had reached the point of believing everything and nothing about him. So I take advantage of this short halt, while Gatsby, so to speak, caught his breath, to clear this set of misconceptions away.

It was a halt, too, in my association with his affairs. For several weeks I didn't see him or hear his voice on the phone – mostly I was in New York, trotting around with Jordan and trying to ingratiate myself with her senile aunt – but finally I went over to his house one Sunday afternoon. I hadn't been there two minutes when somebody brought Tom Buchanan in for a drink. I was startled, naturally, but the really surprising thing was that it hadn't happened before.

They were a party of three on horseback – Tom and a man named Sloane and a pretty woman in a brown riding habit, who had been there previously.

'I'm delighted to see you,' said Gatsby, standing on his porch. 'I'm delighted that you dropped in.'

As though they cared!

'Sit right down. Have a cigarette or a cigar.' He walked around the room quickly, ringing bells. 'I'll have something to drink for you in just a minute.'

He was profoundly affected by the fact that Tom was there. But he would be uneasy anyhow until he had given them something, realising in a vague way that that was all they came for. Mr Sloane wanted nothing. A lemonade? No, thanks. A little champagne? Nothing at all, thanks . . . I'm sorry –

'Did you have a nice ride?'

'Very good roads around here.'

'I suppose the automobiles—'

'Yeah.'

Moved by an irresistible impulse, Gatsby turned to Tom, who had accepted the introduction as a stranger.

'I believe we've met somewhere before, Mr Buchanan.'

'Oh, yes,' said Tom, gruffly polite, but obviously not remembering. 'So we did. I remember very well.'

'About two weeks ago.'

'That's right. You were with Nick here.'

'I know your wife,' continued Gatsby, almost aggressively.

'That so?'

Tom turned to me.

'You live near here, Nick?'

'Next door.'

'That so?'

Mr Sloane didn't enter into the conversation, but lounged back haughtily in his chair; the woman said nothing either – until unexpectedly, after two highballs, she became cordial.

'We'll all come over to your next party, Mr Gatsby,' she suggested. 'What do you say?'

'Certainly; I'd be delighted to have you.'

'Be ver' nice,' said Mr Sloane, without gratitude. 'Well – think ought to be starting home.'

'Please don't hurry,' Gatsby urged them. He had control of himself now, and he wanted to see more of Tom. 'Why don't you – why don't you stay for supper? I wouldn't be surprised if some other people dropped in from New York.'

'You come to supper with me,' said the lady enthusiastically. 'Both of you.'

This included me. Mr Sloane got to his feet.

'Come along,' he said – but to her only.

'I mean it,' she insisted. 'I'd love to have you. Lots of room.'

Gatsby looked at me questioningly. He wanted to go,

and he didn't see that Mr Sloane had determined he shouldn't.

'I'm afraid I won't be able to,' I said.

'Well, you come,' she urged, concentrating on Gatsby.

Mr Sloane murmured something close to her ear.

'We won't be late if we start now,' she insisted aloud.

'I haven't got a horse,' said Gatsby. 'I used to ride in the army, but I've never bought a horse. I'll have to follow you in my car. Excuse me for just a minute.'

The rest of us walked out on the porch, where Sloane and the lady began an impassioned conversation aside.

'My God, I believe the man's coming,' said Tom. 'Doesn't he know she doesn't want him?'

'She says she does want him.'

'She has a big dinner party and he won't know a soul there.' He frowned. 'I wonder where in the devil he met Daisy. By God, I may be old-fashioned in my ideas, but women run around too much these days to suit me. They meet all kinds of crazy fish.'

Suddenly Mr Sloane and the lady walked down the steps and mounted their horses.

'Come on,' said Mr Sloane to Tom, 'we're late. We've got to go.' And then to me: 'Tell him we couldn't wait, will you?'

Tom and I shook hands, the rest of us exchanged a cool nod, and they trotted quickly down the drive, disappearing under the August foliage just as Gatsby, with hat and light overcoat in hand, came out the front door.

Chapter Thirteen

Tom was evidently perturbed at Daisy's running around alone, for on the following Saturday night he came with her to Gatsby's party, although not until later, when the pleasure had finished. It would not have done for him to turn up before. It would not have done at all.

I arrived at the same time, not wanting to take part in that erotic orgy either. Jordan was all I desired and she was spending the evening with a friend so there was nothing to tempt me. I was going purely to please Gatsby, who had asked me himself. I spent a lot of the evening worrying about who this 'friend' Jordan was meeting could be and standing in corners nursing a drink. Jordan's manner towards me had changed of late, but my suspicions would never cease. I knew that she was part of this carnal world but I constantly hoped that she might give it up.

The party was a failure. Perhaps Tom's presence gave the evening its peculiar quality of oppressiveness – it stands out in my memory from Gatsby's other parties that summer. There were the same people, or at least the same sort of people, the same profusion of champagne, the same many-coloured, many-keyed commotion, but I felt an unpleasantness in the air, a pervading harshness that hadn't been there before. Or perhaps I had merely grown used to it, grown to accept West Egg as a world complete in itself, with its own standards and its own great figures, second to nothing because it had no consciousness of being so, and now I was looking at it again, through Daisy's eyes. It is invariably saddening to look through new eyes at things upon which you have expended your own powers of adjustment.

They arrived at twilight, and, as we strolled out among the sparkling hundreds, Daisy's voice was playing murmurous tricks in her throat.

'These things excite me so,' she whispered,'If you want to kiss me any time during the evening, Nick, just let me know and I'll be glad to arrange it for you. Just mention my name. Or present a green card. I'm giving out green—'

'Look around,' suggested Gatsby.

'I'm looking around. I'm having a marvellous—'

'You must see the faces of many people you've heard about.'

Tom's arrogant eyes roamed the crowd.

'We don't go around very much,' he said. 'In fact, I was just thinking I don't know a soul here.'

'Perhaps you know that lady.' Gatsby indicated a gorgeous, scarcely human orchid of a woman who sat in state under a white plum tree. Tom and Daisy stared, with that peculiarly unreal feeling that accompanies the recognition of a hitherto ghostly celebrity of the movies.

'She's lovely,' said Daisy.

'The man bending over her is her director.'

He took them ceremoniously from group to group:

'Mrs Buchanan ... and Mr Buchanan—' After an instant's hesitation he added: 'the polo player.'

'Oh no,' objected Tom quickly, 'not me.'

But evidently the sound of it pleased Gatsby, for Tom remained 'the polo player' for the rest of the evening.

'I've never met so many celebrities!' Daisy exclaimed. 'I liked that man – what was his name? – with the sort of blue nose.'

Gatsby identified him, adding that he was a small producer.

'Well, I liked him anyhow.'

'I'd a little rather not be the polo player,' said Tom pleasantly, 'I'd rather look at all these famous people in – in oblivion.'

Daisy and Gatsby danced. I remember being surprised by his graceful, conservative foxtrot – I had never seen him dance before. Then they sauntered over to my house and sat on the steps for half an hour, while at her request I remained watchfully in the garden. 'In case there's a fire or a flood,' she explained, 'or any act of God.'

Tom appeared from his oblivion as we were sitting down to supper together. 'Do you mind if I eat with some people over here?' he said. 'A fellow's getting off some funny stuff.'

'Go ahead,' answered Daisy genially, 'and if you want to take down any addresses here's my little gold pencil.' She looked around after a moment and told me the girl was 'common but pretty', and I knew that except for the half-hour she'd been alone with Gatsby she wasn't having a good time.

We were at a particularly tipsy table. That was my fault – Gatsby had been called to the phone, and I'd enjoyed these same people only two weeks before. But what had amused me then turned septic on the air now.

'How do you feel, Miss Deker?'

The girl addressed was trying, unsuccessfully, to slump

against my shoulder. At this enquiry she sat up and opened her eyes.

'Wha'?'

A massive and lethargic woman, who had been urging Daisy to play golf with her at the local club tomorrow, spoke in Miss Baedeker's defence:

'Oh, she's all right now. When she's had five or six cocktails she always starts screaming like that. I tell her she ought to leave it alone.'

'I do leave it alone,' affirmed the accused hollowly.

'We heard you yelling, so I said to Doc Civet here: "'There's somebody that needs your help, Doc.'"

'She's much obliged, I'm sure,' said another friend, without gratitude. 'But you got her dress all wet when you stuck her head in the pool.'

'Anything I hate is to get my head stuck in a pool,' mumbled Miss Deker. 'They almost drowned me once over in New Jersey.'

'Then you ought to leave it alone,' countered Dr Civet.

'Speak for yourself!' cried Miss Deker violently. 'Your hand shakes. I wouldn't let you operate on me!'

It was like that. Almost the last thing I remember was standing with Daisy and watching the moving-picture director and his Star. They were still under the white plum tree and their faces were touching except for a pale, thin ray of moonlight between. It occurred to me that he had been very slowly bending towards her all evening to attain this proximity, and even while I watched I saw him stoop one ultimate degree and kiss at her cheek.

'I like her,' said Daisy, 'I think she's lovely.'

But the rest offended her – and inarguably, because it wasn't a gesture but an emotion. She was appalled by West Egg, this unprecedented 'place' that Broadway had begotten upon a Long Island fishing village – appalled by its raw vigour that chafed under the old euphemisms and by the too-obtrusive fate that herded its inhabitants along a short cut from nothing to nothing. She saw something awful in the very simplicity she failed to understand.

I sat on the front steps with them while they waited for their car. It was dark here in front; only the bright door sent ten square feet of light volleying out into the soft black morning. Sometimes a shadow moved against a dressing-room blind above, gave way to another shadow, an indefinite procession of shadows, who rouged and powdered in an invisible glass.

'Who is this Gatsby anyhow?' demanded Tom suddenly. 'Some big bootlegger?'

'Where'd you hear that?' I enquired.

'I didn't hear it. I imagined it. A lot of these newly rich people are just big bootleggers, you know.'

'Not Gatsby,' I said shortly.

He was silent for a moment. The pebbles of the drive crunched under his feet.

'Well, he certainly must have strained himself to get this menagerie together.'

A breeze stirred the grey haze of Daisy's fur collar.

'At least they're more interesting than the people we know,' she said with an effort.

'You didn't look so interested.'

'Well, I was.'

Tom laughed and turned to me.

'Did you notice Daisy's face when that girl asked her to put her under a cold shower?'

Daisy began to sing with the music in a husky, rhythmic whisper, bringing out a meaning in each word that it had never had before and would never have again. When the melody rose, her voice broke up sweetly, following it, in a way contralto voices have, and each change tipped out a little of her warm human magic upon the air.

'Lots of people come who haven't been invited,' she said suddenly. 'That girl hadn't been invited. They simply force their way in and he's too polite to object.'

'I'd like to know who he is and what he does,' insisted Tom. 'And I think I'll make a point of finding out.'

'I can tell you right now,' she answered. 'He owned some drugstores, a lot of drugstores. He built them up himself.'

The dilatory limousine came rolling up the drive.

'Goodnight, Nick,' said Daisy.

Her glance left me and sought the lighted top of the steps, where 'Three o'Clock in the Morning', a neat, sad little waltz of that year, was drifting out the open door. After all, in the very casualness of Gatsby's party there were romantic possibilities totally absent from her world. What was it up there in the song that seemed to be calling her back inside? What would happen now in the dim, incalculable hours? Perhaps some unbelievable guest would arrive, a person infinitely rare and to be marvelled at, some authentically radiant young girl who with one fresh glance at Gatsby, one moment of magical encounter, would blot out those five years of unwavering devotion.

I stayed late that night, Gatsby asked me to wait until he was free, and I lingered in the garden until the inevitable swimming party had run up, chilled and exalted, from the black beach, until the lights were extinguished in the guest rooms overhead. When he came down the steps at last the tanned skin was drawn unusually tight on his face, and his eyes were bright and tired.

'She didn't like it,' he said immediately.

'Of course she did.'

'She didn't like it,' he insisted. 'She didn't have a good time.'

He was silent, and I guessed at his unutterable depression.

'I feel far away from her,' he said. 'It's hard to make her understand.'

'You mean about the dance?'

'The dance?' He dismissed all the dances he had given with a snap of his fingers. 'Old sport, the dance is unimportant.'

He wanted nothing less of Daisy than that she should go to Tom and say: 'I never loved you.' After she had obliterated four years with that sentence they could decide upon the more practical measures to be taken. One of them was that, after she was free, they were to go back to Louisville and be married from her house – just as if it were five years ago.

'And she doesn't understand,' he said. 'She used to be able to understand. We'd sit for hours—'

He broke off and began to walk up and down a desolate

path of fruit rinds and discarded favours and crushed flowers.

'I wouldn't ask too much of her,' I ventured. 'You can't repeat the past.'

'Can't repeat the past?' he cried incredulously. 'Why of course you can!'

He looked around him wildly, as if the past were lurking here in the shadow of his house, just out of reach of his hand.

'I'm going to fix everything just the way it was before,' he said, nodding determinedly. 'She'll see.'

He talked a lot about the past, and I gathered that he wanted to recover something, some idea of himself perhaps, that had gone into loving Daisy. His life had been confused and disordered since then, but if he could once return to a certain starting place and go over it all slowly, he could find out what that thing was . . .

. . . One autumn night, five years before, they had been walking down the street when the leaves were falling, and they came to a place where there were no trees and the sidewalk was white with moonlight. They stopped here and turned towards each other. Now it was a cool night with that mysterious excitement in it which comes at the two changes of the year. The quiet lights in the houses were humming out into the darkness and there was a stir and bustle among the stars. Out of the corner of his eye Gatsby saw that the blocks of the sidewalks really formed a ladder and mounted to a secret place above the trees – he could climb to it, if he climbed alone, and once there he could suck on the pap of life, gulp down the incomparable milk of wonder.

His heart beat faster and faster as Daisy's white face came up to his own. He knew that when he kissed this girl, and for ever wed his unutterable visions to her perishable breath, his mind would never romp again like the mind of God. So he waited, listening for a moment longer to the tuning-fork that had been struck upon a star. Then he kissed her. At his lips' touch she blossomed for him like a flower and the incarnation was complete.

Through all he said, even through his appalling senti-mentality, I was reminded of something – an elusive rhythm, a fragment of lost words, that I had heard some-where a long time ago. For a moment a phrase tried to take shape in my mouth and my lips parted like a dumb man's, as though there was more struggling upon them than a wisp of startled air. But they made no sound, and what I had almost remembered was uncommunicable for ever.

Chapter Fourteen

It was when curiosity about Gatsby was at its highest that the lights in his house failed to go on one Saturday night – and, as obscurely as it had begun, his career as Trimalchio was over. Only gradually did I become aware that the automobiles which turned expectantly into his drive stayed for just a minute and then drove sulkily away. Wondering if he were sick I went over to find out – an unfamiliar butler with a villainous face squinted at me suspiciously from the door.

'Is Mr Gatsby sick?'

'Nope.' After a pause he added 'sir' in a dilatory, grudging way.

'I hadn't seen him around, and I was rather worried. Tell him Mr Carraway came over.'

'Who?' he demanded rudely.

'Carraway.'

'Carraway. All right, I'll tell him.'

Abruptly he slammed the door.

My Finn informed me that Gatsby had dismissed every servant in his house a week ago and replaced them with half a dozen others, who never went into West Egg Village to be bribed by the tradesmen, but ordered moderate supplies over the telephone. The grocery boy reported that the kitchen looked like a pigsty, and the general opinion in the village was that the new people weren't servants at all.

Next day Gatsby called me on the phone.

'Going away?' I enquired.

'No, old sport.'

'I hear you fired all your servants.'

'I wanted somebody who wouldn't gossip. Daisy comes over quite often – in the afternoons.'

So the whole *caravanserai* had fallen in like a card house at the disapproval in her eyes.

'They're some people Wolfsheim wanted to do something for. They're all brothers and sisters. They used to run a small hotel.'

'I see.'

He was calling up at Daisy's request – would I come to lunch at her house tomorrow? Miss Baker would be there.

Half an hour later Daisy herself telephoned and seemed relieved to find that I was coming. Something was up. And yet I couldn't believe that they would choose this occasion for a scene – especially for the rather harrowing scene that Gatsby had outlined in the garden.

The next day was boiling, almost the last, certainly the warmest, of the summer. As my train emerged from the tunnel into sunlight, only the hot whistles of the National Biscuit Company broke the simmering hush at noon. The straw seats of the car hovered on the edge of combustion; the woman next to me perspired delicately for a while into her white shirtwaist, and then, as her newspaper dampened under her fingers, lapsed despairingly into deep heat with a desolate cry. Her pocketbook slapped to the floor.

'Oh, my!' she gasped.

I picked it up with a weary bend and handed it back to her, holding it at arm's length and by the extreme tip of the corners to indicate that I had no designs upon it – but everyone nearby, including the woman, suspected me just the same.

'Hot!' said the conductor to familiar faces. 'Some weather! Hot! Hot! Hot! Is it hot enough for you? Is it hot? Is it . . . ?'

My commutation ticket came back to me with a dark stain from his hand. That anyone should care in this heat whose flushed lips he kissed, whose head made damp the pyjama pocket over his heart!

Through the hall of the Buchanans' house blew a faint wind, carrying the sound of the telephone bell out to Gatsby and me as we waited at the door.

'The master's body!' roared the butler into the mouth-piece. 'I'm sorry, madame, but we can't furnish it – it's far too hot to touch this noon!'

What he really said was: 'Yes . . . yes . . . I'll see.'

He set down the receiver and came towards us, glisten-ing slightly, to take our stiff straw hats.

'Madame expects you in the salon!' he cried, needlessly indicating the direction. In this heat every extra gesture was an affront to the common store of life.

The room, shadowed well with awnings, was dark and cool. Daisy and Jordan lay upon an enormous couch, like silver idols weighing down their own white dresses against the singing breeze of the fans.

'We can't move,' they said together.

Jordan's fingers, powdered white over their tan, rested for a moment in mine. Her grey eyes slid to my own, and in them was a hidden warmth that made me smile. Her white dress was conservative and alluring. The high neck only served to amplify her large breasts and the design hugged her waist, falling in a white cascade to just above her knee, which, when she sat down, slid seductively up her thigh, revealing curved, golden muscles.

I realised that I had been gazing at her too long and I hastily turned away, enquiring in a hushed tone, 'And Mr Thomas Buchanan, the athlete?'

Simultaneously I heard his voice, gruff, muffled, husky, at the hall telephone.

Gatsby stood in the centre of the crimson carpet and gazed around with fascinated eyes. Daisy watched him and laughed, her sweet, exciting laugh; a tiny gust of powder rose from her bosom into the air.

'The rumour is,' whispered Jordan, 'that that's Tom's girl on the telephone.'

We were silent and I was surprised to see that Daisy appeared not to care at all.

The voice in the hall rose high with annoyance: 'Very well, then, I won't sell you the car at all . . . I'm under no obligations to you at all . . . and as for your bothering me about it at lunchtime, I won't stand that at all!'

'Holding down the receiver,' said Daisy cynically.

'No, he's not,' I assured her. 'It's a bona-fide deal. I happen to know about it.'

Tom flung open the door, blocked out its space for a moment with his thick body, and hurried into the room.

'Mr Gatsby!' He put out his broad, flat hand with well-concealed dislike. 'I'm glad to see you, sir . . . Nick . . . '

'Make us a cold drink,' cried Daisy.

As he left the room again she got up and went over to Gatsby and pulled his face down, kissing him on the mouth. I blushed and looked away.

'You know I love you,' she murmured.

'You forget there's a lady present,' said Jordan.

Daisy looked around doubtfully.

'You kiss Nick too. In fact far worse I've heard about—'

'What a low, vulgar girl!'

My face reddened all the more. I suppose I was naive to think that Jordan wouldn't tell Daisy about us, but I felt a secret part of me exposed all the same.

'I don't care!' cried Daisy, and began to clog on the brick fireplace. Then she remembered the heat and sat down guiltily on the couch just as a freshly laundered nurse leading a little girl came into the room.

'Bles-sed pre-cious,' she crooned, holding out her arms. 'Come to your own mother that loves you.'

The child, relinquished by the nurse, rushed across the room and rooted shyly into her mother's dress.

'The bles-sed pre-cious! Did Mother get powder on your old yellowy hair? Stand up now, and say – How-de-do.'

Gatsby and I in turn leaned down and took the small, reluctant hand. Afterwards he kept looking at the child with surprise. I don't think he had ever really believed in its existence before.

'I got dressed before luncheon,' said the child, turning eagerly to Daisy.

'That's because your mother wanted to show you off.' Her face bent into the single wrinkle of the small, white neck. 'You dream, you. You absolute little dream.'

'Yes,' admitted the child calmly. 'Aunt Jordan's got on a white dress too.'

'How do you like Mother's friends?' Daisy turned her around so that she faced Gatsby. 'Do you think they're pretty?'

'Where's Daddy?'

'She doesn't look like her father,' explained Daisy. 'She looks like me. She's got my hair and shape of the face.'

Daisy sat back upon the couch. The nurse took a step forwards and held out her hand.

'Come, Pammy.'

'Goodbye, sweetheart!'

With a reluctant backward glance the well-disciplined child held to her nurse's hand and was pulled out the door, just as Tom came back, preceding four gin rickeys that clicked full of ice.

Gatsby took up his drink.

'They certainly look cool,' he said, with visible tension.

We drank in long, greedy swallows.

'I read somewhere that the sun's getting hotter every year,' said Tom genially. 'It seems that pretty soon the earth's going to fall into the sun – or wait a minute – it's just the opposite – the sun's getting colder every year.'

'Come outside,' he suggested to Gatsby, 'I'd like you to have a look at the place.'

I went with them out to the veranda. On the green Sound, stagnant in the heat, one small sail crawled slowly towards the fresher sea. Gatsby's eyes followed it momentarily; he raised his hand and pointed across the bay.

'I'm right across from you.'

'So you are.'

Our eyes lifted over the rose-beds and the hot lawn and the weedy refuse of the dog days alongshore. Slowly the white wings of the boat moved against the blue cool limit of the sky. Ahead lay the scalloped ocean and the abounding blessed isles.

'There's sport for you,' said Tom, nodding. 'I'd like to be out there with him for about an hour.'

We had luncheon in the dining room, darkened too against the heat, and drank down nervous gaiety with the cold ale.

'What'll we do with ourselves this afternoon?' cried Daisy, 'and the day after that, and the next thirty years?'

'Don't be morbid,' Jordan said. 'Life starts all over again when it gets crisp in the fall.'

I glanced over at her in surprise but her expression gave nothing away. She had sounded cold and hard just then, like she held no tie to this summer and would be glad to see the back of it.

'But it's so hot,' insisted Daisy, on the verge of tears, 'and everything's so confused. Let's all go to town!'

Her voice struggled on through the heat, beating against it, moulding its senselessness into forms.

'I've heard of making a garage out of a stable,' Tom was saying to Gatsby, 'but I'm the first man who ever made a stable out of a garage.'

'Who wants to go to town?' demanded Daisy insistently.

Gatsby's eyes floated towards her.

'Ah,' she cried, 'you look so cool.'

Their eyes met, and they stared together at each other, alone in space. With an effort she glanced down at the table.

'You always look so cool,' she repeated.

She had told him that she loved him, and Tom Buchanan saw. He was astounded. His mouth opened a little, and he looked at Gatsby, and then back at Daisy as if he had just recognised her as someone he knew a long time ago.

'You resemble the advertisement of the man,' she went on innocently. 'You know the advertisement of the man—'

'All right,' broke in Tom quickly, 'I'm perfectly willing to go to town. Come on – we're all going to town.'

He got up, his eyes still flashing between Gatsby and his wife. No one moved.

'Come on!' His temper cracked a little. 'What's the matter, anyhow? If we're going to town, let's start. Let's start out now.'

His hand, trembling with his effort at self-control, bore to his lips the last of his glass of ale. Daisy's voice got us to our feet and out on to the blazing gravel drive.

'Are we just going to go?' she objected. 'Like this? Aren't we going to let anyone smoke a cigarette first? That would be better.'

'Everybody smoked all through lunch.'

'Oh, let's have fun,' she begged him. 'It's too hot to fuss. Let's have fun!'

He didn't answer.

'Have it your own way,' she said. 'Come on, Jordan.'

She turned to go upstairs and get ready, while Tom and Gatsby made to go outside and wait. Jordan caught my eye just as I was about to follow them. She tilted her head upwards and winked, before disappearing in a shiver of white.

I paused a moment, uncertain.

'I'm just going to ... be a minute,' I said to the retreating backs.

Tom didn't even turn around but merely grunted consent.

Gatsby said nothing.

Relatively sure that they did not suspect me, I traced Jordan's flight up the stairs and on to the landing. My heart was beginning to beat an ecstatic rhythm in my chest and the incessant heat made my palms sweaty. She was standing in the doorway of one of the bedrooms, leaning languidly against the frame.

'I thought you might be a little too hot waiting for us outside,' she said in a husky tone.

'That was kind of you. Where's Daisy?'

'Getting ready elsewhere.'

Jordan sashayed into the bedroom and I followed her, closing the door. It was a vast and faceless room, much like any other that I had seen in the house. The furniture was expensive and bland. The decor was fashionable and opaque. There was an empty picture frame on a side table.

'Did you want to speak to me?' I asked.

'I didn't have a lot of speaking in mind.'

I gulped hard and wiped the crystal beads of sweat that had burst on my forehead.

'I owe you,' she added.

'You don't owe me anything.'

Her cat-like eyes surveyed me with interest, calculating my honesty.

'What about last time?'

'It's not an eye for an eye.'

She shrugged. Then she reached her arms above her head and stretched, displaying her lithe, pert body. It reminded me of the first time that I had met her at this very house when she had prowled into my life on a humid, dusky evening. She had changed me and I hoped that I had changed her too.

'Why Nick, you look almost sentimental.'

'Is that a crime?'

'It's for fools.'

She held the edges of her dress and slid it over her head in a fluid movement, shaking out her dark hair and sighing deeply, as if released. She placed the dress carefully on the bed and then stretched again before me in her underwear.

I felt myself go hard and the beating of my heart quickened.

'Did you wear that just for me?' I deadpanned desperately, nodding towards her bra.

She regarded me coolly. This was a game that was not to be made fun of.

'You look beautiful,' I added because it was the truth and because I wanted to appease her.

'Sentimental,' she scolded, but her eyes told me otherwise.

She strutted over to me, her breasts bobbing in the confines of her bra and her hips swaying like a pendulum. I enveloped her in my arms as she reached me and she melted into my embrace.

'I'm so hot,' she gushed breathlessly in my ear. 'I'm so dreadfully hot.'

I ran my hands down her damp back to the curve of her buttocks. Stroking it over her smooth, tight underwear. I felt myself pulse and my head grew dizzy. The heat and the smell of Jordan's body – sweet and salty like caramel – made my throat dry with longing. Yearning uncoiled in the pit of my stomach and surged through my limbs. I was filled with a fiery heat that quivered my nerves and heightened my senses.

She brought her lips to mine, their full silkiness pressing against my own and working in a slow, gentle rhythm. I closed my eyes and succumbed to my heady desire, relishing the taste of her and flicking my tongue through her parted lips for more. Holding her tight, I pushed my erection against her. She cupped my chin and rubbed my stubble as I moved my hands through her dark, soft hair.

My hunger for her intensified as she dipped her tongue inside my mouth in return and tickled the skin at the back of my neck with her fingers. My chest heaved with the pent-up rush of longing that surged through me and I raked my fingers through her hair. Thrusting her hips against mine, she began undoing the buttons of my shirt. I pulled away from her lips and began trailing kisses across her neck and chest, my hands roaming to her behind, stroking her cheeks. She moaned softly and pulled back my shirt. Kissing me between my pecs, she stepped away from me.

'Wait,' she whispered as I went to take her in my arms again.

She walked over to a dresser and picked up a wooden hand mirror. As she brought it over to me, her lips curved in a sly smile.

'What do you think?'

I stared at her blankly.

She turned the hand mirror over so that the plain, wooden back was upwards and then she gently clapped it against her hand.

'See?'

'No.'

'You do.' After a moment of silence she muttered angrily, 'Oh, Nick . . .'

I couldn't bear not to have her and so I reached across and pulled her back to me. I prised the hand mirror from her grasp and said, 'Bend over.'

She giggled. 'No, you won't know what to do. I'll do it first.'

My cheeks flushed but I didn't stop her as she took the hand mirror back and began unbuckling my belt. Once I was in my underwear, she told me to bend over and lean my elbows on the bed. I obeyed.

I had a vaguely, faint, sick feeling curdling in my stomach, but I tried to ignore it. I wanted Jordan more than anything, even if it was on her terms. Her white dress was laid out on the bed before me and I stared at it while she moved herself into position. I could feel the warmth of her body still radiating from it and the intoxicating scent of her still lingered in its folds.

Suddenly, I felt a sharp slap on my behind. A jolt of pain sliced my body, I gasped and yet . . . there was a remaining buzz of pleasure that took me by surprise. Just as I recognised it, she slapped me again, producing a second blow of pain intermingled with burning pleasure. I groaned softly. She hit me again and again, getting harder and faster, and then she stopped.

I felt her tongue licking up my spine and between my shoulder blades to the sensitive, soft skin at the back of my neck. I gasped, shuddering in delight and she smacked me again. Thrills coursed through me as she hit me again and again. A beautiful mixture of pain and pleasure rushed over me as she slapped me harder and faster until, suddenly, she stopped.

She leaned over me and lightly bit my earlobe. I realised

I was panting and my hands were knotted into the bed sheets.

'My turn,' she whispered, nuzzling my neck.

Placing the hand mirror in front of me, she unclasped her bra and let her full breasts fall on to her ribs in plump curves. My erection pulsed with longing and she bent over beside me, smiling.

'Not too hard,' she whispered.

I stood behind her, the hand mirror in my hot sweaty palm and her pert backside clad in peach underwear spread before me. I reached forwards and gently stroked it before patting her with the hand mirror.

'Nick, not like—'

I smacked her harder and she shuddered with pleasure. I hit her several more times until I could see rivulets of sweat coursing down her back and her limbs quivering with excitement. To give her such pain and pleasure thrilled me and I relished our mutual power. I smacked her harder and faster and harder and faster, until I didn't think that I could take any more.

Throwing the hand mirror down, I pulled her to me. She clasped her hands behind my neck and kissed me earnestly, tugging my bottom lip between her teeth. We kissed, grasped and groped each other, our breath dragging through our pounding chests and our bodies slick with sweat. The air was humid and thick. The afternoon was silent save for our moaning and groaning and I vaguely hoped that Daisy hadn't gone downstairs yet or else the others would be suspecting us.

Jordan dragged down my underwear and I ripped off her own, rubbing and stroking the wetness between her legs. She convulsed against the bed, sinking her nails into my chest and gasping. I plunged my fingers inside her and she cried out with pleasure as I moved them in slow circles. Taking my erection in her hands, she began to tug and pull me.

Unable to withhold my violent lust any longer, I slid my hand around the golden arch of her hip to the small of her back, lifting her off the bed and pushing myself inside her. She gasped. As I thrust into her, my hands skimmed her ribs and took each of her breasts into my palms. I licked, kissed and nipped her while my hands rubbed her nipples until they were hard and erect.

She threw back her head as I pounded into her and I groaned as an intense thrill built in my stomach, threatening to overflow. My hips thudded against her own and I clenched my teeth in unbelievable pleasure. A hot, raw feeling was forming and I squeezed my eyes shut as the bliss grew stronger and stronger. I thrust faster and harder, faster and harder, until I was overcome, and climaxed with a cry of sweet relief. I collapsed over Jordan, who was panting hard.

'Nick,' she whispered, blowing a gush of air through her red, puckered lips.

I was unable to speak. My head rang with pleasure and my ears roared with the intense blast of my orgasm. I simply held her and wallowed in a warm, fuzzy glow that had enveloped my body.

Jordan wriggled and shifted slightly under me and for a moment I thought she was going to pull away in the disinterested manner she usually did. But instead she hesitantly kissed my chin. I was unable to stop myself from smiling and her cheeks reddened with embarrassment. It was clear that she wasn't used to being romantic. She pulled away from me then and went to wash herself off, looking distinctly uncomfortable.

I stayed on the bed a while longer, still overcome, but more pleased by her sweet, sincere kiss. After my breath had returned to normal, I sat up and watched as she approached me holding a pot of cream.

'It's for the sore,' she said. 'Put some on me?'

She turned around and offered up her firm, red behind.

I took a blob of the cool, smooth cream and spread it across the raw area.

Jordan sighed. 'That feels so good,' she whispered.

I gently rubbed and pressed it into her, massaging her plump cheeks as I did so.

'I think you're enjoying that,' she said with a husky laugh.

She stepped away and took the cream off me. 'Your turn.'

I rolled over and let her soothe me. The balm was cool and rich and I was practically falling asleep under her skilled, firm touch when she said, 'Nick? I'm done now.'

She laughed again as I turned around and yawned.

'See, sometimes you like the things you try.'

I grinned and staggered to my feet, pulling her to me. She seemed a little surprised as I kissed her lightly and without lust on the mouth and then watched her a while, drinking her in. She began to look uncomfortable again and shrugged me off.

'You had better go down and let me get ready. The others will be wondering where you are.'

I nodded at no one in particular and began putting my clothes back on, trying to ignore my sweat-drenched skin. I winced as I pulled up my pants, realising for the first time just how sore my behind actually was. The thought of sitting for another handful of hours on a hard chair did not seem very appealing.

Meanwhile, Jordan was powdering herself by the dresser and fixing her hair. She wasn't looking at me and I felt that she was nervous.

'You can leave now,' she said in a tight voice.

Fastening her underwear back in place, she began smoothing out the bed sheets.

'I can help,' I said, picking up the hand mirror and passing it to her.

'No,' she replied firmly. 'I can do it myself.'

She stopped suddenly. 'Look, it's broken,' she said, turning the hand mirror over to show me the shattered glass. 'That's bad luck.'

Chapter Fifteen

I emerged into the glaring sun to see two men shuffling hot pebbles with their feet. They did not appear to care where I'd been so I made no explanation and silently joined them. A silver curve of the moon hovered already in the western sky. I hated to wonder what the conversation had been like before I reappeared; they seemed to be doing a fine job of ignoring each other and we were left in this bank of silence for a while. Daisy was taking an awful long time, or perhaps Jordan had asked her to. I did not understand their ways, but I hoped that one or both of them would appear soon.

Gatsby started to speak, changed his mind, but not before Tom wheeled and faced him expectantly.

'Have you got your stables here?' asked Gatsby with an effort.

'About a quarter of a mile down the road.'

'Oh.'

A pause.

'I don't see the idea of going to town,' broke out Tom savagely. 'Women get these notions in their heads—'

'Shall we take anything to drink?' called Daisy from an upper window.

'I'll get some whiskey,' answered Tom. He went inside.

Gatsby turned to me rigidly:

'I can't say anything in his house, old sport.'

'She's got an indiscreet voice,' I remarked. 'It's full of—' I hesitated.

'Her voice is full of money,' he said suddenly.

That was it. I'd never understood before. It was full of money – that was the inexhaustible charm that rose and fell in it, the jingle of it, the cymbals' song of it . . . high in a white palace the king's daughter, the golden girl . . .

Tom came out of the house wrapping a quart bottle in a towel, followed by Daisy and Jordan wearing small tight hats of metallic cloth and carrying light capes over their arms. Jordan didn't even glance at me when we met, as if she had forgotten that only moments before she had been groaning and writhing in my arms. I suppose you wouldn't have thought it to look at her; as neat and smart as anything, and maybe she didn't think it. Perhaps the beauty of it was that she never thought it so no one else did – not her golfing opponents, not her silly old aunt and not the rest of West Egg.

'Shall we all go in my car?' suggested Gatsby. He felt the hot, green leather of the seat. 'I ought to have left it in the shade.'

'Is it standard shift?' demanded Tom.

'Yes.'

'Well, you take my coupé and let me drive your car to town.'

The suggestion was distasteful to Gatsby.

'I don't think there's much gas,' he objected.

'Plenty of gas,' said Tom boisterously. He looked at the gauge. 'And if it runs out I can stop at a drugstore. You can buy anything at a drugstore nowadays.'

A pause followed this apparently pointless remark. Daisy looked at Tom, frowning, and an indefinable expression, at once definitely unfamiliar and vaguely recognisable, as if I had only heard it described in words, passed over Gatsby's face.

'Come on, Daisy,' said Tom, pressing her with his hand towards Gatsby's car. 'I'll take you in this circus wagon.'

He opened the door, but she moved out from the circle of his arm.

'You take Nick and Jordan. We'll follow you in the coupé.'

She walked close to Gatsby, touching his coat with her hand. Jordan and Tom and I got into the front seat of Gatsby's car, Tom pushed the unfamiliar gears tentatively, and we shot off into the oppressive heat, leaving them out of sight behind.

'Did you see that?' demanded Tom.

'See what?'

He looked at me keenly, realising that Jordan and I must have known all along.

'You think I'm pretty dumb, don't you?' he suggested. 'Perhaps I am, but I have a – almost a second sight, some-times, that tells me what to do. Maybe you don't believe that, but science—'

He paused. The immediate contingency overtook him, pulled him back from the edge of the theoretical abyss.

'I've made a small investigation of this fellow,' he con-tinued. 'I could have gone deeper if I'd known—'

'Do you mean you've been to a medium?' inquired Jordan humorously, her husky voice cutting in.

'What?' Confused, he stared at us as we laughed. 'A medium?'

'About Gatsby.'

'About Gatsby! No, I haven't. I said I'd been making a small investigation of his past.'

'And you found he was an Oxford man,' said Jordan helpfully.

'An Oxford man!' He was incredulous. 'Like hell he is! He wears a pink suit.'

'Nevertheless he's an Oxford man.'

'Oxford, New Mexico,' snorted Tom contemptuously, 'or something like that.'

'Listen, Tom. If you're such a snob, why did you invite him to lunch?' demanded Jordan crossly.

'Daisy invited him; she knew him before we were married – God knows where!'

We were all irritable now with the fading ale, and aware of it we drove for a while in silence. Then as Dr T. J. Eckleburg's faded eyes came into sight down the road, I remembered Gatsby's caution about gasoline.

'We've got enough to get us to town,' said Tom.

'But there's a garage right here,' objected Jordan. 'I don't want to get stalled in this baking heat.' Tom threw on both brakes impatiently, and we slid to an abrupt dusty stop under Wilson's sign. After a moment the proprietor emerged from the interior of his establishment and gazed hollow-eyed at the car.

'Let's have some gas!' cried Tom roughly. 'What do you think we stopped for – to admire the view?'

'I'm sick,' said Wilson without moving. 'Been sick all day.'

'What's the matter?'

'I'm all run down.'

'Well, shall I help myself?' Tom demanded. 'You sounded well enough on the phone.'

With an effort Wilson left the shade and support of the doorway and, breathing hard, unscrewed the cap of the tank. In the sunlight his face was green.

'I didn't mean to interrupt your lunch,' he said. 'But I need money pretty bad, and I was wondering what you were going to do with your old car.'

'How do you like this one?' enquired Tom. 'I bought it last week.'

'It's a nice yellow one,' said Wilson, as he strained at the handle.

'Like to buy it?'

'Big chance,' Wilson smiled faintly. 'No, but I could make some money on the other.'

'What do you want money for, all of a sudden?'

'I've been here too long. I want to get away. My wife and I want to go West.'

'Your wife does,' exclaimed Tom, startled.

'She's been talking about it for ten years.' He rested for

a moment against the pump, shading his eyes. 'And now she's going whether she wants to or not. I'm going to get her away.'

The coupé flashed by us with a flurry of dust and the flash of a waving hand.

'What do I owe you?' demanded Tom harshly.

'I just got wised up to something funny the last two days,' remarked Wilson. 'That's why I want to get away. That's why I been bothering you about the car.'

'What do I owe you?'

'Dollar twenty.'

The relentless beating heat was beginning to confuse me and I had a bad moment there before I realised that so far his suspicions hadn't alighted on Tom. He had discovered that Myrtle had some sort of life apart from him in another world, and the shock had made him physically sick. I stared at him and then at Tom, who had made a parallel discovery less than an hour before – and it occurred to me that there was no difference between men, in intelligence or race, so profound as the difference between the sick and the well. Wilson was so sick that he looked guilty, unforgivably guilty – as if he had just got some poor girl with child.

'I'll let you have that car,' said Tom. 'I'll send it over tomorrow afternoon.'

That locality was always vaguely disquieting, even in the broad glare of afternoon, and now I turned my head as though I had been warned of something behind. Over the ash heaps the giant eyes of Dr T. J. Eckleburg kept their vigil, but I perceived, after a moment, that other eyes were regarding us with peculiar intensity from less than twenty feet away.

In one of the windows over the garage the curtains had been moved aside a little, and Myrtle Wilson was peering down at the car. So engrossed was she that she had no consciousness of being observed, and one emotion after another crept into her face like objects into a slowly developing picture. Her expression was curiously familiar – it was an expression I had often seen on women's faces, but on Myrtle Wilson's face it seemed purposeless and inexplicable until I realised that her eyes, wide with jealous terror, were fixed not on Tom, but on Jordan Baker, whom she took to be his wife.

There is no confusion like the confusion of a simple mind, and as we drove away Tom was feeling the hot whips of panic. His wife and his mistress, until an hour ago secure and inviolate, were slipping precipitately from his control. Instinct made him step on the accelerator with the double purpose of overtaking Daisy and leaving Wilson behind, and we sped along towards Astoria at fifty miles an hour, until, among the spidery girders of the elevated, we came in sight of the easy-going blue coupé.

'Those big movies around Fiftieth Street are cool,' suggested Jordan. 'I love New York on summer afternoons when everyone's away. There's something very sensuous about it – overripe, as if all sorts of funny fruits were going to fall into your hands.'

The word 'sensuous' had the effect of further disquieting Tom, but before he could invent a protest the coupé came to a stop, and Daisy signalled us to draw up alongside.

'Where are we going?' she cried.

'How about the movies?'

'It's so hot,' she complained. 'You go. We'll ride around and meet you after.' With an effort her wit rose faintly. 'We'll meet you on some corner. I'll be the man smoking two cigarettes.'

'We can't argue about it here,' Tom said impatiently, as a truck gave out a cursing whistle behind us. 'You follow me to the south side of Central Park, in front of the Plaza.'

Several times he turned his head and looked back for their car, and if the traffic delayed them he slowed up until they came into sight. I think he was afraid they would dart down a side street and out of his life for ever.

But they didn't. And we all took the less explicable step of engaging the parlour of a suite in the Plaza Hotel.

The prolonged and tumultuous argument that ended by herding us into that room eludes me, though I have a sharp physical memory that, in the course of it, my underwear kept climbing like a damp snake around my legs and intermittent beads of sweat raced cool across my back. The notion originated with Daisy's suggestion that we hire five bathrooms and take cold baths, and then assumed more tangible form as 'a place to have a mint julep'. Each of us said over and over that it was a 'crazy idea' – we all talked at once to a baffled clerk and thought, or pretended to think, that we were being very funny . . .

The room was large and stifling, and, though it was already four o'clock, opening the windows admitted only a gust of hot shrubbery from the Park. Daisy went to the mirror and stood with her back to us, fixing her hair.

'It's a swell suite,' whispered Jordan respectfully, and everyone laughed.

'Open another window,' commanded Daisy, without turning around.

'There aren't any more.'

'Well, we'd better telephone for an axe—'

'The thing to do is to forget about the heat,' said Tom impatiently. 'You make it ten times worse by crabbing about it.'

He unrolled the bottle of whiskey from the towel and put it on the table.

'Why not let her alone, old sport?' remarked Gatsby. 'You're the one that wanted to come to town.'

There was a moment of silence. The telephone book slipped from its nail and splashed to the floor, whereupon Jordan whispered, 'Excuse me' – but this time no one laughed.

'I'll pick it up,' I offered.

'I've got it.' Gatsby examined the parted string, muttered 'Hum!' in an interested way, and tossed the book on a chair.

'That's a great expression of yours, isn't it?' said Tom sharply.

'What is?'

'All this "old sport" business. Where'd you pick that up?'

'Now see here, Tom,' said Daisy, turning around from the mirror, 'if you're going to make personal remarks I won't stay here a minute. Call up and order some ice for the mint julep.'

As Tom took up the receiver the compressed heat exploded into sound and we were listening to the portentous chords of Mendelssohn's 'Wedding March' from the ballroom below.

'Imagine marrying anybody in this heat!' cried Jordan dismally.

'Still – I was married in the middle of June,' Daisy remembered, 'Louisville in June! Somebody fainted. Who was it fainted, Tom?'

'Biloxi,' he answered shortly.

'A man named Biloxi. "Blocks" Biloxi, and he made boxes – that's a fact – and he was from Biloxi, Tennessee.'

'They carried him into my house,' appended Jordan, 'because we lived just two doors from the church. And he stayed three weeks, until Daddy told him he had to get out. The day after he left Daddy died.' After a moment she added as if she might have sounded irreverent, 'There wasn't any connection.'

'I used to know a Bill Biloxi from Memphis,' I remarked.

'That was his cousin. I knew his whole family history before he left. He gave me an aluminum putter that I use today.'

The music had died down as the ceremony began and

now a long cheer floated in at the window, followed by intermittent cries of 'Yea-ea-ea!' and finally by a burst of jazz as the dancing began.

'We're getting old,' said Daisy. 'If we were young we'd rise and dance.'

'Remember Biloxi,' Jordan warned her. 'Where'd you know him, Tom?'

'Biloxi?' He concentrated with an effort. 'I didn't know him. He was a friend of Daisy's.'

'He was not,' she denied. 'I'd never seen him before. He came down in the private car.'

'Well, he said he knew you. He said he was raised in Louisville. Asa Bird brought him around at the last minute and asked if we had room for him.'

Jordan smiled.

'He was probably bumming his way home. He told me he was president of your class at Yale.'

Tom and I looked at each other blankly.

'Biloxi?'

'First place, we didn't have any president—'

Gatsby's foot beat a short, restless tattoo and Tom eyed him suddenly.

'By the way, Mr Gatsby, I understand you're an Oxford man.'

'Not exactly.'

'Oh, yes, I understand you went to Oxford.'

'Yes – I went there.'

A pause. Then Tom's voice, incredulous and insulting: 'You must have gone there about the time Biloxi went to New Haven.'

Another pause. A waiter knocked and came in with crushed mint and ice but the silence was unbroken by his 'thank you' and the soft closing of the door. This tremendous detail was to be cleared up at last.

'I told you I went there,' said Gatsby.

'I heard you, but I'd like to know when.'

'It was in 1919, I only stayed five months. That's why I can't really call myself an Oxford man.'

Tom glanced around to see if we mirrored his unbelief. But we were all looking at Gatsby.

'It was an opportunity they gave to some of the officers after the Armistice,' he continued. 'We could go to any of the universities in England or France.'

I wanted to get up and slap him on the back. I had one of those renewals of complete faith in him that I'd experienced before.

Daisy rose, smiling faintly, and went to the table.

'Open the whiskey, Tom,' she ordered, 'and I'll make you

a mint julep. Then you won't seem so stupid to yourself . . . Look at the mint!'

'Wait a minute,' snapped Tom, 'I want to ask Mr Gatsby one more question.'

'Go on,' Gatsby said politely.

'What kind of a row are you trying to cause in my house anyhow?'

They were out in the open at last and Gatsby was content.

'He isn't causing a row.' Daisy looked desperately from one to the other. 'You're causing a row. Please have a little self-control.'

'Self-control!' Repeated Tom incredulously. 'I suppose the latest thing is to sit back and let Mr Nobody from Nowhere make love to your wife. Well, if that's the idea you can count me out . . . Nowadays people begin by sneering at family life and family institutions, and next they'll throw everything overboard and have intermarriage between black and white.'

Flushed with his impassioned gibberish, he saw himself standing alone on the last barrier of civilisation.

'We're all white here,' murmured Jordan.

'I know I'm not very popular. I don't give big parties. I suppose you've got to make your house into a pigsty in order to have any friends – in the modern world.'

Angry as I was, as we all were, I was tempted to laugh whenever he opened his mouth. The transition from libertine to prig was so complete.

'I've got something to tell you, old sport—' began Gatsby.

But Daisy guessed at his intention.

'Please don't!' she interrupted helplessly. 'Please let's all go home. Why don't we all go home?'

'That's a good idea.' I got up. 'Come on, Tom. Nobody wants a drink.'

'I want to know what Mr Gatsby has to tell me.'

'Your wife doesn't love you,' said Gatsby. 'She's never loved you. She loves me.'

'You must be crazy!' exclaimed Tom automatically.

Gatsby sprang to his feet, vivid with excitement.

'She never loved you, do you hear?' he cried. 'She only married you because I was poor and she was tired of waiting for me. It was a terrible mistake, but in her heart she never loved anyone except me!'

At this point Jordan and I tried to go, but Tom and Gatsby insisted with competitive firmness that we remain – as though neither of them had anything to conceal and it would be a privilege to partake vicariously of their emotions.

'Sit down, Daisy,' Tom's voice groped unsuccessfully for the paternal note. 'What's been going on? I want to hear all about it.'

'I told you what's been going on,' said Gatsby. 'Going on for five years – and you didn't know.'

Tom turned to Daisy sharply.

'You've been seeing this fellow for five years?'

'Not seeing,' said Gatsby. 'No, we couldn't meet. But both of us loved each other all that time, old sport, and you didn't know. I used to laugh sometimes' – but there was no laughter in his eyes – 'to think that you didn't know.'

Tom tapped his thick fingers together like a clergyman and leaned back in his chair. 'You're crazy!' he exploded. 'I can't speak about what happened five years ago, because I didn't know Daisy then – and I'll be damned if I see how you got within a mile of her unless you brought the groceries to the back door. But all the rest of that's a goddamned lie. Daisy loved me when she married me and she loves me now.'

'No,' said Gatsby, shaking his head.

'She does, though. The trouble is that sometimes she gets foolish ideas in her head and doesn't know what she's doing.' He nodded sagely. 'And what's more, I love Daisy too. Once in a while I go off on a spree and make a fool of myself, but I always come back, and in my heart I love her all the time.'

'You're revolting,' said Daisy. She turned to me, and her voice, dropping an octave lower, filled the room with thrilling scorn: 'Do you know why we left Chicago? I'm surprised that they didn't treat you to the story of that little spree.'

'And this man's better?' Tom burst out. 'Do you know what he houses? Do you know what happens in that grotesque mansion of his? Day and Night. I heard rumours of such a thing in nightclubs – of a new place people could go, but I didn't think it could be true. And that is the man you make love to?'

Daisy's face quivered a little, but this was not news to her. 'I know it all. Jay has told me everything,' she said quietly. 'He never partook in any of those . . . things.'

'What difference does that make?'

'It makes every kind of difference!' interjected Gatsby. 'It's not a thing to be ashamed of, it's not like your cheating and lies.'

'Don't speak about things that you don't understand!' yelled Tom. He turned on Jordan and me, his fists clenched. 'Do you know the sordid things this man does?'

We stared at him and neither of us spoke. He must

have read it from our expressions because he wrinkled his nose.

'Nick, I didn't think you had it in you,' he muttered and I felt unjustly ashamed.

Gatsby walked across the room and stood beside Daisy.

'It's all over now,' he said to her earnestly. 'It doesn't matter any more. Just tell him the truth – that you never loved him – and it's all wiped out for ever.'

She looked at him blindly. 'Why – how could I love him – possibly?'

'You never loved him.'

She hesitated. Her eyes fell on Jordan and me with a sort of appeal, as though she realised at last what she was doing – and as though she had never, all along, intended doing anything at all. But it was done now. It was too late.

'I never loved him,' she said, with perceptible reluctance.

'Not at Kapiolani?' demanded Tom suddenly.

'No.'

From the ballroom beneath, muffled and suffocating chords were drifting up on hot waves of air.

'Not that day I carried you down from the Punch Bowl to keep your shoes dry?' There was a husky tenderness in his tone . . . 'Daisy?'

'Please don't.' Her voice was cold, but the rancour was

gone from it. She looked at Gatsby. 'There, Jay,' she said – but her hand as she tried to light a cigarette was trembling. Suddenly she threw the cigarette and the burning match on the carpet.

'Oh, you want too much!' she cried to Gatsby. 'I love you now – isn't that enough? I can't help what's past.' She began to sob helplessly. 'I did love him once – but I loved you too.'

Gatsby's eyes opened and closed.

'You loved me too?' he repeated.

'Even that's a lie,' said Tom savagely. 'She didn't know you were alive. Why – there're things between Daisy and me that you'll never know, things that neither of us can ever forget.'

The words seemed to bite physically into Gatsby.

'I want to speak to Daisy alone,' he insisted. 'She's all excited now—'

'Even alone I can't say I never loved Tom,' she admitted in a pitiful voice. 'It wouldn't be true.'

'Of course it wouldn't,' agreed Tom.

She turned to her husband.

'As if it mattered to you,' she said.

'Of course it matters. I'm going to take better care of you from now on.'

'You don't understand,' said Gatsby, with a touch of panic. 'You're not going to take care of her any more.'

'I'm not?' Tom opened his eyes wide and laughed. He could afford to control himself now. 'Why's that?'

'Daisy's leaving you.'

'Nonsense.'

'I am, though,' she said with a visible effort.

'She's not leaving me!' Tom's words suddenly leaned down over Gatsby. 'Certainly not for a common swindler who'd have to steal the ring he put on her finger.'

'I won't stand this!' cried Daisy. 'Oh, please let's get out.'

'Who are you, anyhow?' broke out Tom. 'You're one of that bunch that hangs around with Meyer Wolfsheim – that much I happen to know. I've made a little investigation into your affairs – and I'll carry it further to-morrow.'

'You can suit yourself about that, old sport.' said Gatsby steadily.

'I found out what your "drugstores" were.' He turned to us and spoke rapidly. 'He and this Wolfsheim bought up a lot of side-street drugstores here and in Chicago and sold grain alcohol over the counter. That's one of his little stunts. I picked him for a bootlegger the first time I saw him, and I wasn't far wrong.'

'What about it?' said Gatsby politely. 'I guess your friend Walter Chase wasn't too proud to come in on it.'

'And you left him in the lurch, didn't you? You let him go to jail for a month over in New Jersey. God! You ought to hear Walter on the subject of you.'

'He came to us dead broke. He was very glad to pick up some money, old sport.'

'Don't you call me "old sport"!' cried Tom.

Gatsby said nothing.

'Walter could have you up on the betting laws too, but Wolfsheim scared him into shutting his mouth.'

That unfamiliar yet recognisable look was back again in Gatsby's face.

'That drugstore business was just small change,' continued Tom slowly, 'but you've got something on now that Walter's afraid to tell me about.'

I glanced at Daisy, who was staring terrified between Gatsby and her husband, and at Jordan, who had begun to balance an invisible but absorbing object on the tip of her chin. Then I turned back to Gatsby – and was startled at his expression. He looked – and this is said in all contempt for the babbled slander of his garden – as if he had 'killed a man'. For a moment the set of his face could be described in just that fantastic way.

It passed, and he began to talk excitedly to Daisy, denying everything, defending his name against accusations that had not been made. But with every word she was drawing further and further into herself, so he gave that up, and only the dead dream fought on as the afternoon slipped away, trying to touch what was no longer tangible, struggling unhappily, undespairingly, towards that lost voice across the room.

The voice begged again to go.

'Please, Tom! I can't stand this any more.'

Her frightened eyes told that whatever intentions, whatever courage, she had had, were definitely gone.

'You two start on home, Daisy,' said Tom. 'In Mr Gatsby's car.'

She looked at Tom, alarmed now, but he insisted with magnanimous scorn.

'Go on. He won't annoy you. I think he realises that his presumptuous little flirtation is over.'

They were gone, without a word, snapped out, made accidental, isolated, like ghosts, even from our pity.

After a moment Tom got up and began wrapping the unopened bottle of whiskey in the towel.

'Want any of this stuff? Jordan? . . . Nick?'

I didn't answer.

'Nick?' he asked again.

'What?'

'Want any?'

'No . . . I just remembered that today's my birthday.'

I was thirty. Before me stretched the portentous, menacing road of a new decade.

Tom appeared not to hear me. 'I'm getting in the car anyhow,' he said, striding out of the room.

It was just Jordan and I then and the air was close.

'Happy birthday,' she purred.

She closed the space between us and kissed me lightly on the cheek. She smelled of power and talcum, and her lips looked their usual pillowy softness but for some reason I didn't feel them. I blinked at her.

'Know what Daisy will do?' she asked.

'What?'

'Nothing.'

I gazed at the empty table and thought of Gatsby, staring at a green light on a dock.

'You don't know what.'

'I do.'

'She loves him. She said so herself, you heard her.'

'Love?' she scoffed.

'It's an emotion that people feel.'

Jordan evidently didn't like the turn of this conversation because she clapped her hands together and treated me to a wicked grin, saying, 'You, Nick, need a spanking.' And she clapped her hands together some more and looked scornful and cold. 'Harder, harder,' she giggled, turning away and flouncing out the room. 'Harder!'

Perhaps it was the heat or the fight or the earlier spanking, but I suddenly felt sick.

Chapter Sixteen

It was seven o'clock when we got into the coupé with Tom and started for Long Island. He talked incessantly, exulting and laughing, but his voice was as remote from Jordan and me as the foreign clamour on the sidewalk or the tumult of the elevated overhead. Human sympathy has its limits, and we were content to let all their tragic arguments fade with the city lights behind. Thirty – the promise of a decade of loneliness, a thinning list of single men to know, a thinning briefcase of enthusiasm, thinning hair.

But there was Jordan beside me, who, unlike Daisy, was too wise ever to carry well-forgotten dreams from age to age. As we passed over the dark bridge her beautiful face fell lazily against my coat's shoulder and the formidable stroke of thirty died away with the reassuring pressure of her hand. I forgave her for earlier. I reminded myself that I loved her, because I did love her. I thought of nobody else but her after all and what better example of love was there than that? With her warm curved body resting against my own, I wanted to be nowhere else in the world.

So we drove on towards death through the cooling twilight.

The young Greek, Michaelis, who ran the coffee joint beside the ash heaps was the principal witness at the inquest. He had slept through the heat until after five, when he strolled over to the garage, and found George Wilson sick in his office – really sick, pale as his own pale hair and shaking all over. Michaelis advised him to go to bed, but Wilson refused, saying that he'd miss a lot of business if he did. While his neighbour was trying to persuade him a violent racket broke out overhead.

'I've got my wife locked in up there,' explained Wilson calmly. 'She's going to stay there till the day after tomorrow, and then we're going to move away.'

Michaelis was astonished; they had been neighbours for four years, and Wilson had never seemed faintly capable of such a statement. Generally he was one of these worn-out men: when he wasn't working, he sat on a chair in the doorway and stared at the people and the cars that passed along the road. When anyone spoke to him he invariably laughed in an agreeable, colourless way. He was his wife's man and not his own.

So naturally Michaelis tried to find out what had happened, but Wilson wouldn't say a word – instead he began to throw curious, suspicious glances at his visitor and ask him what he'd been doing at certain times on certain days. Just as the latter was getting uneasy, some workmen came past the door bound for his restaurant, and Michaelis took the opportunity to get away, intending to come back later. But he didn't. He supposed he forgot to, that's all. When he came outside again, a little after seven, he was reminded of the conversation because he heard Mrs Wilson's voice, loud and scolding, downstairs in the garage.

'Beat me!' he heard her cry. 'Throw me down and beat me, you dirty little coward!'

A moment later she rushed out into the dusk, waving her hands and shouting – before he could move from his door the business was over.

The 'death car' as the newspapers called it, didn't stop; it came out of the gathering darkness, wavered tragically for a moment, and then disappeared around the next bend. Michaelis wasn't even sure of its colour – he told the first policeman that it was light green. The other car, the one going towards New York, came to rest a hundred yards beyond, and its driver hurried back to where Myrtle Wilson, her life violently extinguished, knelt in the road and mingled her thick dark blood with the dust.

Michaelis and this man reached her first, but when they had torn open her shirtwaist, still damp with perspiration, they saw that her left breast was swinging loose like a flap, and there was no need to listen for the heart beneath. The mouth was wide open and ripped at the corners, as though she had choked a little in giving up the tremendous vitality she had stored so long.

We saw the three or four automobiles and the crowd when we were still some distance away.

'Wreck!' said Tom. 'That's good. Wilson'll have a little business at last.'

He slowed down, but still without any intention of stopping, until, as we came nearer, the hushed, intent faces of the people at the garage door made him automatically put on the brakes.

'We'll take a look,' he said doubtfully, 'just a look.'

I became aware now of a hollow, wailing sound which issued incessantly from the garage, a sound which as we got out of the coupé and walked towards the door resolved itself into the words 'Oh, my God!' uttered over and over in a gasping moan.

'There's some bad trouble here,' said Tom excitedly.

He reached up on tiptoes and peered over a circle of heads into the garage, which was lit only by a yellow light in a swinging wire basket overhead. Then he made a harsh sound in his throat, and with a violent thrusting movement of his powerful arms pushed his way through.

The circle closed up again with a running murmur of expostulation; it was a minute before I could see anything at all. Then new arrivals deranged the line, and Jordan and I were pushed suddenly inside.

Myrtle Wilson's body, wrapped in a blanket, and then in another blanket, as though she suffered from a chill in the hot night, lay on a work-table by the wall, and Tom, with his back to us, was bending over it, motionless. Next to him stood a motorcycle policeman taking down names with much sweat and correction in a little book. At first I couldn't find the source of the high, groaning words that echoed clamorously through the bare garage – then I saw Wilson standing on the raised threshold of his office, swaying back and forth and holding to the doorposts with both hands. Some man was talking to him in a low voice and attempting, from time to time, to lay a hand on his shoulder, but Wilson neither heard nor saw. His eyes would drop slowly from the swinging light to the laden table by the wall, and then jerk back to the light again, and he gave out incessantly his high, horrible call:

'Oh, my Ga-od! Oh, my Ga-od! Oh, Ga-od! Oh, my Ga-od!'

Presently Tom lifted his head with a jerk and, after staring around the garage with glazed eyes, addressed a mumbled incoherent remark to the policeman.

'M-a-y-,' the policeman was saying, '-o—'

'No, r-,' corrected the man, 'M-a-v-r-o—'

'Listen to me!' muttered Tom fiercely.

'r,' said the policeman, 'o—'

'g—'

'g –' He looked up as Tom's broad hand fell sharply on his shoulder. 'What you want, fella?'

'What happened? – that's what I want to know.'

'Auto hit her. Ins'antly killed.'

'Instantly killed,' repeated Tom, staring.

'She ran out ina road. Son of a bitch didn't even stopus car.'

'There was two cars,' said Michaelis, 'one comin', one goin', see?'

'Going where?' asked the policeman keenly.

'One goin' each way. Well, she,' – his hand rose towards the blankets but stopped halfway and fell to his side – 'she ran out there an' the one comin' from N'york knock right into her, goin' thirty or forty miles an hour.'

'What's the name of this place here?' demanded the officer.

'Hasn't got any name.'

A pale well-dressed negro stepped near.

'It was a yellow car,' he said, 'big yellow car. New.'

'See the accident?' asked the policeman.

'No, but the car passed me down the road, going faster'n forty. Going fifty, sixty.'

'Come here and let's have your name. Look out now. I want to get his name.'

Some words of this conversation must have reached Wilson, swaying in the office door, for suddenly a new theme found voice among his gasping cries:

'You don't have to tell me what kind of car it was! I know what kind of car it was!'

Watching Tom, I saw the wad of muscle at the back of his shoulder tighten under his coat. He walked quickly over to Wilson and, standing in front of him, seized him firmly by the upper arms.

'You've got to pull yourself together,' he said with sooth- ing gruffness.

Wilson's eyes fell upon Tom; he started up on his tiptoes

and then would have collapsed to his knees had not Tom held him upright.

'Listen,' said Tom, shaking him a little. 'I just got here a minute ago, from New York. I was bringing you that coupé we've been talking about. That yellow car I was driving this afternoon wasn't mine – do you hear? I haven't seen it all afternoon.'

Only the negro and I were near enough to hear what he said, but the policeman caught something in the tone and looked over with truculent eyes.

'What's all that?' he demanded.

'I'm a friend of his.' Tom turned his head but kept his hands firm on Wilson's body. 'He says he knows the car that did it ... it was a yellow car.'

Some dim impulse moved the policeman to look suspiciously at Tom.

'And what colour's your car?'

'It's a blue car, a coupé.'

'We've come straight from New York,' I said.

Someone who had been driving a little behind us confirmed this, and the policeman turned away.

'Now, if you'll let me have that name again correct –' Picking up Wilson like a doll, Tom carried him into the office, set him down in a chair, and came back.

'If somebody'll come here and sit with him,' he snapped authoritatively. He watched while the two men standing closest glanced at each other and went unwillingly into the room. Then Tom shut the door on them and came down the single step, his eyes avoiding the table. As he passed close to me he whispered: 'Let's get out.'

Self-consciously, with his authoritative arms breaking the way, we pushed through the still gathering crowd, passing a hurried doctor, case in hand, who had been sent for in wild hope half an hour ago.

Tom drove slowly until we were beyond the bend – then his foot came down hard, and the coupé raced along through the night. In a little while I heard a low husky sob, and saw that the tears were overflowing down his face.

'The goddamned coward!' he whimpered. 'He didn't even stop his car.'

The Buchanans' house floated suddenly towards us through the dark rustling trees. Tom stopped beside the porch and looked up at the second floor, where two windows bloomed with light among the vines.

'Daisy's home,' he said.

As we got out of the car he glanced at me and frowned slightly.

'I ought to have dropped you in West Egg, Nick. There's nothing we can do tonight.'

A change had come over him, and he spoke gravely, and with decision. As we walked across the moonlight gravel to the porch he disposed of the situation in a few brisk phrases.

'I'll telephone for a taxi to take you home, and while you're waiting you and Jordan better go in the kitchen and have them get you some supper – if you want any.' He opened the door. 'Come in.'

'No, thanks. But I'd be glad if you'd order me the taxi. I'll wait outside.'

Jordan put her hand on my arm.

'Won't you come in, Nick?'

'No, thanks.'

I was feeling a little sick and I wanted to be alone. But Jordan lingered.

'It's only half-past nine,' she said.

I'd be damned if I'd go in; I'd had enough of all of them for one day, and suddenly that included Jordan too.

'Daisy will want to be by herself,' Jordan added. 'I'll have the whole night free.'

I stared at her stupidly.

She reached across and stroked my cheek in what she

245

thought was a seductive fashion and tried to lock her eyes on mine. I felt a stab of hatred then and it took me by surprise. I instantly buried it, reassuring myself that I was tired and shocked and tired some more. I couldn't hate Jordan Baker, my Jordan Baker – that was inconceivable.

'Who knows what we could do in a whole night,' she attempted to purr.

I felt a twinge. It sounded crass and sick in this empty night.

She ran her hand down my chest to my crotch where she traced the line of my waistband, smiling eagerly.

'Do you think of nothing else?'

It took me a moment to realise that I had spoken.

Jordan snatched her hand back. I had rejected her.

'Such a gentlemen,' she hissed.

Turning abruptly away, she ran up the porch steps into the house.

I sat down for a few minutes with my head in my hands, until I heard the phone taken up inside and the butler's voice calling a taxi. Then I walked slowly down the drive away from the house, intending to wait by the gate.

I hadn't gone twenty yards when I heard my name and Gatsby stepped from between two bushes into the path. I must have felt pretty weird by that time, because I could think of nothing except the luminosity of his pink suit under the moon.

'What are you doing?' I enquired.

'Just standing here, old sport.'

Somehow, that seemed a despicable occupation. For all I knew he was going to rob the house in a moment; I wouldn't have been surprised to see sinister faces, the faces of 'Wolfsheim's people', behind him in the dark shrubbery.

'Did you see any trouble on the road?' he asked after a minute.

'Yes.'

He hesitated.

'Was she killed?'

'Yes.'

'I thought so; I told Daisy I thought so. It's better that the shock should all come at once. She stood it pretty well.'

He spoke as if Daisy's reaction was the only thing that mattered.

'I got to West Egg by a side road,' he went on, 'and left the car in my garage. I don't think anybody saw us, but of course I can't be sure.'

I disliked him so much by this time that I didn't find it necessary to tell him he was wrong.

'Who was the woman?' he enquired.

'Her name was Wilson. Her husband owns the garage. How the devil did it happen?'

'Well, I tried to swing the wheel—' He broke off, and suddenly I guessed at the truth.

'Was Daisy driving?'

'Yes,' he said after a moment, 'but of course I'll say I was. You see, when we left New York she was very nervous and she thought it would steady her to drive – and this woman rushed out at us just as we were passing a car coming the other way. It all happened in a minute, but it seemed to me that she wanted to speak to us, thought we were somebody she knew. Well, first Daisy turned away from the woman towards the other car, and then she lost her nerve and turned back. The second my hand reached the wheel I felt the shock – it must have killed her instantly.'

'It ripped her open—'

'Don't tell me, old sport.' He winced. 'Anyhow – Daisy stepped on it. I tried to make her stop, but she couldn't, so I pulled on the emergency brake. Then she fell over into my lap and I drove on.

'She'll be all right tomorrow,' he said presently. 'I'm just going to wait here and see if he tries to bother her about that unpleasantness this afternoon. She's locked herself into her room, and if he tries any brutality she's going to turn the light out and on again.'

'He won't touch her,' I said. 'He's not thinking about her.'

'I don't trust him, old sport.'

'How long are you going to wait?'

'All night, if necessary. Anyhow, till they all go to bed.'

A new point of view occurred to me. Suppose Tom found out that Daisy had been driving. He might think he saw a connection in it – he might think anything. I looked at the house; there were two or three bright windows downstairs and the pink glow from Daisy's room on the second floor.

'You wait here,' I said. 'I'll see if there's any sign of a commotion.'

I walked back along the border of the lawn, traversed the gravel softly, and tiptoed up the veranda steps. The drawing-room curtains were open, and I saw that the room was empty. Crossing the porch where we had dined that June night three months before, I came to a small rectangle of light which I guessed was the pantry window. The blind was drawn, but I found a rift at the sill.

Daisy and Tom were sitting opposite each other at the kitchen table, with a plate of cold fried chicken between them, and two bottles of ale. He was talking intently across the table at her, and in his earnestness his hand had fallen upon and covered her own. Once in a while she looked up at him and nodded in agreement.

They weren't happy, and neither of them had touched the chicken or the ale – and yet they weren't unhappy either. There was an unmistakable air of natural intimacy about the picture, and anybody would have said that they were conspiring together.

As I tiptoed from the porch I heard my taxi feeling its way along the dark road towards the house. Gatsby was waiting where I had left him in the drive.

'Is it all quiet up there?' he asked anxiously.

'Yes, it's all quiet.' I hesitated. 'You'd better come home and get some sleep.'

He shook his head.

'I want to wait here till Daisy goes to bed. Goodnight, old sport.'

He put his hands in his coat pockets and turned back eagerly to his scrutiny of the house, as though my presence marred the sacredness of the vigil. So I walked away and left him standing there in the moonlight – watching over nothing.

Chapter Seventeen

I couldn't sleep all night; a foghorn was groaning incessantly on the Sound, and I tossed half-sick between grotesque reality and savage, frightening dreams. Towards dawn I heard a taxi go up Gatsby's drive, and immediately I jumped out of bed and began to dress – I felt that I had something to tell him, something to warn him about, and morning would be too late.

Crossing his lawn, I saw that his front door was still open and he was leaning against a table in the hall, heavy with dejection or sleep.

'Nothing happened,' he said wanly. 'I waited, and about four o'clock she came to the window and stood there for a minute and then turned out the light.'

His house had never seemed so enormous to me as it did that night when we hunted through the great rooms for cigarettes. We pushed aside curtains that were like pavilions, and felt over innumerable feet of dark wall for electric light switches – once I tumbled with a sort of splash upon the keys of a ghostly piano. There was an inexplicable amount of dust everywhere, and the rooms were musty, as though they hadn't been aired for many days. I found the humidor on an unfamiliar table, with two stale, dry cigarettes inside. Throwing open the French windows of the drawing room, we sat smoking out into the darkness.

'You ought to go away,' I said. 'It's pretty certain they'll trace your car.'

'Go away now, old sport?'

'Go to Atlantic City for a week, or up to Montreal.'

He wouldn't consider it. He couldn't possibly leave Daisy until he knew what she was going to do. He was clutching at some last hope and I couldn't bear to shake him free.

It was this night that he told me the strange story of his youth with Dan Cody – told it to me because 'Jay Gatsby' had broken up like glass against Tom's hard malice, and the long secret extravaganza was played out. I think that he would have acknowledged anything now, without reserve, but he wanted to talk about Daisy.

She was the first 'nice' girl he had ever known. In various unrevealed capacities he had come in contact with such people, but always with indiscernible barbed wire between. He found her excitingly desirable. He went to her house, at first with other officers from Camp Taylor, then alone. It amazed him – he had never been in such a beautiful house before. But what gave it an air of breathless intensity, was that Daisy lived there – it was as casual a thing to her as his tent out at camp was to him. There was a ripe mystery about it, a hint of bedrooms upstairs more beautiful and cool than other bedrooms, of gay and radiant activities taking place through its corridors, and of romances that were not musty and laid away already in lavender but fresh and breathing and redolent of this year's shining motor cars and of dances whose flowers were scarcely withered. It excited him, too, that many men had already loved Daisy – it increased her value in his eyes. He felt their presence all about the house, pervading the air with the shades and echoes of still-vibrant emotions.

But he knew that he was in Daisy's house by a colossal accident. However glorious might be his future as Jay Gatsby, he was at present a penniless young man without a past, and at any moment the invisible cloak of his uniform might slip from his shoulders. So he made the most of his time. He took what he could get, ravenously and unscrupulously – eventually he took Daisy one still

October night, took her because he had no real right to touch her hand.

He might have despised himself, for he had certainly taken her under false pretences. I don't mean that he had traded on his phantom millions, but he had deliberately given Daisy a sense of security; he let her believe that he was a person from much the same stratum as herself – that he was fully able to take care of her. As a matter of fact, he had no such facilities — he had no comfortable family standing behind him, and he was liable at the whim of an impersonal government to be blown anywhere about the world.

But he didn't despise himself and it didn't turn out as he had imagined. He had intended, probably, to take what he could and go – but now he found that he had committed himself to the following of a grail. He knew that Daisy was extraordinary, but he didn't realise just how extraordinary a 'nice' girl could be. She vanished into her rich house, into her rich, full life, leaving Gatsby – nothing. He felt married to her, that was all.

When they met again, two days later, it was Gatsby who was breathless, who was, somehow, betrayed. Her porch was bright with the bought luxury of star-shine; the wicker of the settee squeaked fashionably as she turned towards him and he kissed her curious and lovely mouth. She had caught a cold, and it made her voice huskier and more charming than ever, and Gatsby was overwhelmingly aware of the youth and mystery that wealth imprisons and preserves, of the freshness of many clothes, and of Daisy, gleaming like silver, safe and proud above the hot struggles of the poor.

'I can't describe to you how surprised I was to find out I loved her, old sport. I even hoped for a while that she'd throw me over, but she didn't, because she was in love with me too. She thought I knew a lot because I knew different things from her ... Well, there I was, 'way off my ambitions, getting deeper in love every minute, and all of a sudden I didn't care. What was the use of doing great things if I could have a better time telling her what I was going to do?'

On the last afternoon before he went abroad, he sat with Daisy in his arms for a long, silent time. It was a cold fall day, with fire in the room and her cheeks flushed. Now and then she moved and he changed his arm a little, and once he kissed her shining hair. The afternoon had made them tranquil for a while, as if to give them a deep memory for the long parting the next day promised. They had never been closer in their month of love, nor communicated more profoundly one with another, than when she brushed silent lips against his coat's shoulder or when he touched the end of her fingers, gently, as though she were asleep.

He did extraordinarily well in the war. He was a captain before he went to the front, and following the Argonne battles he got his majority and the command of the divisional machine-guns. After the Armistice he tried frantically to get home, but some complication or misunderstanding sent him to Oxford instead. He was worried now – there was a quality of nervous despair in Daisy's letters. She didn't see why he couldn't come. She was feeling the pressure of the world outside, and she wanted to see him and feel his presence beside her and be reassured that she was doing the right thing after all.

For Daisy was young and her artificial world was redolent of orchids and pleasant, cheerful snobbery and orchestras which set the rhythm of the year, summing up the sadness and suggestiveness of life in new tunes. All night the saxophones wailed the hopeless comment of the 'Beale Street Blues' while a hundred pairs of golden and silver slippers shuffled the shining dust. At the grey tea hour there were always rooms that throbbed incessantly with this low, sweet fever, while fresh faces drifted here and there like rose petals blown by the sad horns around the floor.

Through this twilight universe Daisy began to move again

with the season; suddenly she was again keeping half a dozen dates a day with half a dozen men, and drowsing asleep at dawn with the beads and chiffon of an evening dress tangled among dying orchids on the floor beside her bed. And all the time something within her was crying for a decision. She wanted her life shaped now, immediately – and the decision must be made by some force – of love, of money, of unquestionable practicality – that was close at hand.

That force took shape in the middle of spring with the arrival of Tom Buchanan. There was a wholesome bulkiness about his person and his position, and Daisy was flattered. Doubtless there was a certain struggle and a certain relief. The letter reached Gatsby while he was still at Oxford.

It was dawn now on Long Island and we went about opening the rest of the windows downstairs, filling the house with grey-turning, gold-turning light. The shadow of a tree fell abruptly across the dew and ghostly birds began to sing among the blue leaves. There was a slow, pleasant movement in the air, scarcely a wind, promising a cool, lovely day.

'I don't think she ever loved him.' Gatsby turned around from a window and looked at me challengingly. 'You must remember, old sport, she was very excited this afternoon. He told her those things in a way that frightened her – that made it look as if I was some kind of cheap sharper. And the result was she hardly knew what she was saying.'

He sat down gloomily.

'Of course she might have loved him just for a minute, when they were first married – and loved me more even then, do you see?'

Suddenly he came out with a curious remark.

'In any case,' he said, 'it was just personal.'

What could you make of that, except to suspect some intensity in his conception of the affair that couldn't be measured?

He came back from France when Tom and Daisy were still on their wedding trip, and made a miserable but irresistible journey to Louisville on the last of his army pay. He stayed there a week, walking the streets where their footsteps had clicked together through the November night and revisiting the out-of-the-way places to which they had driven in her white car. Just as Daisy's house had always seemed to him more mysterious and gay than other houses, so his idea of the city itself, even though she was gone from it, was pervaded with a melancholy beauty.

He left feeling that if he had searched harder, he might have found her – that he was leaving her behind. The daycoach – he was penniless now – was hot. He went out to the open vestibule and sat down on a folding-chair, and the station slid away and the backs of unfamiliar buildings moved by. Then out into the spring fields, where a yellow trolley raced them for a minute with people in it who might once have seen the pale magic of her face along the casual street.

The track curved and now it was going away from the sun, which, as it sank lower, seemed to spread itself in benediction over the vanishing city where she had drawn her breath. He stretched out his hand desperately as if to snatch only a wisp of air, to save a fragment of the spot that she had made lovely for him. But it was all going by too fast now for his blurred eyes and he knew that he had lost that part of it, the freshest and the best, for ever.

It was nine o'clock when we finished breakfast and went out on the porch. The night had made a sharp difference in the weather and there was an autumn flavour in the air. The gardener, the last one of Gatsby's former servants, came to the foot of the steps.

'I'm going to drain the pool today, Mr Gatsby. Leaves'll start falling pretty soon, and then there's always trouble with the pipes.'

'Don't do it today,' Gatsby answered. He turned to me apologetically. 'You know, old sport, I've never used that pool all summer?'

I looked at my watch and stood up.

'Twelve minutes to my train.'

I didn't want to go to the city. I wasn't worth a decent stroke of work, but it was more than that – I didn't want to leave Gatsby. I missed that train, and then another, before I could get myself away.

'I'll call you up,' I said finally.

'Do, old sport.'

'I'll call you about noon.'

We walked slowly down the steps.

'I suppose Daisy'll call too.' He looked at me anxiously, as if he hoped I'd corroborate this.

'I suppose so.'

'Well, goodbye.'

We shook hands and I started away. Just before I reached the hedge I remembered something and turned around.

'They're a rotten crowd,' I shouted across the lawn. 'You're worth the whole damn bunch put together.'

I've always been glad I said that. It was the only compliment I ever gave him, because I disapproved of him from beginning to end. First he nodded politely, and then his face broke into that radiant and understanding smile, as if we'd been in ecstatic cahoots on that fact all the time. His gorgeous pink rag of a suit made a bright spot of colour against the white steps, and I thought of the night when I first came to his ancestral home, three months before. The lawn and drive had been crowded with the faces of those who guessed at his corruption – and he had stood on those steps, concealing his incorruptible dream, as he waved them goodbye.

I thanked him for his hospitality. We were always thanking him for that – I and the others.

'Goodbye,' I called. 'I enjoyed breakfast, Gatsby.'

Up in the city, I tried for a while to list the quotations on an interminable amount of stock, then I fell asleep in my swivel-chair. The phone woke me, and I started up with sweat breaking out on my forehead. It was Jordan Baker; she often called me up because the uncertainty of her own movements between hotels and clubs and private houses made her hard to find in any other way. Usually her voice came over the wire as something fresh and cool and husky, as if a divot from a green golf links had come sailing in at the office window, but this morning it seemed harsh and dry.

'I've left Daisy's house,' she said. 'I'm at Hempstead, and I'm going down to Southampton this afternoon.'

Probably it had been tactful to leave Daisy's house, but the act annoyed me, and her next remark made me rigid.

'You weren't so nice to me last night.'

'How could it have mattered then?'

Silence for a moment. Then:

'However – I want to see you. Suppose I don't go to Southampton? You should come to my aunt's house this afternoon. She's out. Yes?'

Something had changed. I was slightly reluctant to go. I could feel it and Jordan could hear it but we both ignored it. I wasn't sure what this change in me was or where it had come from.

'All right,' I said and put down the phone.

I settled matters at the office and caught a taxi to Jordan's aunt's house. As I drew up, I noticed that the curtains of the front room were already drawn and for some unknown reason, I felt remarkably weary.

When I climbed out of the car, I realised that some of the hot mugginess of the day before had abated and I stood still for a moment, relishing the sun on my face – my tired, weary face – as the taxi petered out in the distance. I lost myself for a while in the sun's yellow glaring glaze and if it wasn't for catching the twitch of curtains from the corner of my eye, then I believe I would have stayed there longer. The sun had been bright and dazzling almost all summer, but I hadn't noticed it, I had only felt the heat and the oppression.

I told myself that I would move in a minute. The twitch of curtains meant that Jordan had spotted me and would be waiting for me, but I wanted to stay here for just a few more uninterrupted moments.

I heard a door open and saw Jordan standing on the porch nearby, watching me.

'Come in, Nick, before someone sees you.'

I didn't want to follow her husky voice into the shadowed darkness, but I did.

She led me to the front room again and I took off my jacket.

'It's not like you to be so quiet.'

I suppose I had just come from the office and still felt somewhat businesslike.

'I'm sorry ... I'm tired.'

'Shall I get us some drinks?'

Without waiting for a reply, she fluttered away. She was wearing those wide-leg pants again, but this time her blouse was tawny, like her beautiful skin – golden like caramel and honey and money.

She reappeared what felt like an age later with two iced glasses of something. I don't know what it was because I didn't touch mine, I just held it in my hand and felt old. Too old for this.

'I'm sorry about last night,' I said.

We had been sitting in silence.

This seemed to bring Jordan to life. Her chin dipped and her grey eyes grew haughty with some of their previous burning light.

'I wouldn't usually invite someone here again who had treated me like that. It was bad form, it was ... disgraceful.'

And I almost wanted to laugh because Jordan Baker calling bad manners disgraceful was so very funny. But I didn't laugh, I clutched my iced something and nodded stoically.

'I am very sorry. It won't happen again.'

She nodded stiffly and clenched her jaw.

'But why did you invite me here?' I asked.

'What do you mean?'

'Why am I here and not your graduate?'

At first she began to protest and flick her dark hair about and say that she didn't know what graduate I was talking about, but at last she came straight.

'I like you, Nick.'

It was a lie and she said it because she knew it was what I wanted to hear, but I believed her for that moment. I wanted to believe her and so I did. I put down my iced something and I strode across the room. I pulled her into my arms and scooped her up.

'Nick! Wha—!' she began, spilling her drink and dropping the glass on a cushion.

I carried her out of the front room and up the stairs. It was lighter here and I kicked open the door of a room and found a bed inside. I pressed her on it, feeling the warmth of the sun's rays that filtered through the window.

I began kissing her and she kissed me back with all the passion and burning desire that she had. I slowed her down. I wanted to take the time to taste her properly. With steady deliberation, I moved my mouth against hers. I licked her lips and sucked her tongue and all with gentle, slow care. She fought me at first, trying to make me harder and faster, but I didn't give in.

Our bodies melted into one another and it was bliss. I began kissing her cheeks and then her neck and then her chest. Her skin was beautifully soft and its honey-colour shone like polished gold in the bright sunlight. I ran my fingers through her dark, smouldering hair, feeling its tendrils slip from my grasp and I felt the warmth of her whole body pressed up against mine on the bed.

'Nick, you should—'

But I silenced her with a gentle kiss, taking her plump bottom lip between my teeth and biting it slowly. I didn't want props or games or anything apart from just her. I slid my fingers over the undulations of her skin, tickling her. She giggled breathlessly in my ear before sucking and nipping my earlobe, which sent indulgent sparks of pleasure fizzing through my body. I moved my hips against hers in tender, gradual thrusts and was rewarded by a velvety groan escaping her lips.

She glided her hands down my chest and slipped them beneath my shirt, stroking the skin of my belly. Her fingers traced the line of hair that trailed from my navel to my waistband, caressing the warm skin. Tugging on the hair gently, she undid my pants and pulled them down. In turn, I began unbuttoning her blouse, carefully this time, and I lifted her gently off the bed to tug it off.

I began kissing her neck, before moving down her chest, between her breasts, to the top of her pants. I undid them and licked the dainty skin beneath, dipping my tongue into her navel. She wriggled and giggled, trying to push me off.

'That tickles!'

I did it again, this time trailing my tongue across the firm bumps of her toned abdominals. She gasped and giggled and pulled my hips closer to hers clamping her lips to mine. I kissed her and pulled away, taking off her pants and then peeling down her underwear. She watched me, her grey, sun-stained eyes glazed with the scorching heat of longing.

I hitched her legs over my shoulders and then slowly and deliberately kissed from her knee up the inside of her right leg. She shivered as I did so, yearning for satisfaction. I paused as I reached her hips and gently blew on her, watching her writhe, and then I dipped my head between her legs and licked her. She gasped as I slowly and gently worked my tongue on her, relishing her sweet, succulent taste. As her passion grew, I began to work harder and faster, until her body was bowing with pleasure.

I stopped and began kissing her thighs again as she panted against the sheets of the bed. Suddenly, she sat up and rolled me over so that she was on top. She pulled down my underwear and ripped off my shirt, running her nails across my skin. I gasped as she tickled the tender area at the tops of my thighs and then bent over, taking my erection in her hands and bringing the tip to her mouth.

Locking her eyes on mine, she twirled her tongue around the tip of me, sending darts of hot pleasure shooting up my body. Lightly she sucked me, encasing my erection in her red lips and flicking her tongue backwards and forwards. When I thought that I couldn't take any more, she took all of me into her mouth and sucked hard. My body jerked and twisted with joy. Fiery heat curdled in my lower stomach and the pressure in my groin began to intensify. Just as I thought that I was going to come, she stopped and grinned at me.

I panted, my chest heaving with pent-up pleasure and my head numb and dizzy. Jordan stood and reached behind her back, unclasping her bra. Her beautiful, full breasts fell on to her slight ribcage and she leaned over me. I felt her erect nipples brush the skin on my chest as she bent closer and then she planted a hard, long kiss on my lips. She pulled away and grinned again.

I inched my hands around to her smooth strong back, letting my fingers glide down her skin to the curved plumpness of her behind. There I clasped and grasped her, pressing her closer to me. She kissed and licked my neck, returning my fervent thrusts, and suddenly she arched her back so that I was pushed inside her.

I gasped at her warm wetness and felt my pleasure quickly beginning to build once more. She clinched her strong, golden thighs around my waist and rhythmically thrust into me, each push a stab of amazing bliss. I moved my hands to her chest and began massaging and squeezing her breasts. I circled her erect nipples with the tip of my index finger, watching as she threw back her head, letting her hair snake down her back.

She groaned to the ceiling and began moving faster and

harder, pumping into me. Pressure formed within my stomach once more and I clenched my teeth as great waves of blistering desire surged over me again and again. Jordan moved harder and faster and harder and faster until I didn't think that I could take any more. Her hips thudded against mine and she leaned back, increasing the deep angle.

Suddenly, her mouth fell open and she dug her nails into my shoulders, raking them across my chest. She cried out a scream of ecstasy and fell against me, whispering my name, and her body was limp and damp. In that same moment, I came, my intense pleasure rushing through my body and ringing every nerve with an electric thrill. My ears roared with the force of it and I collapsed against the sheets, my heart and body wrung to nothing.

We lay still for a while, just panting and raw. My head was high and fizzing with the after-effect of a deep satisfaction I had never felt before so I scarcely knew what I was doing when I wrapped my arms around Jordan, hugging her to me. She fidgeted and wriggled uncomfortably and I quickly let her go. Raising herself on to her elbows, she looked at me with smug, playful eyes.

'Did you enjoy that?' she asked.

I didn't want to be part of her cold, bereft games any longer so I didn't reply.

She ran a finger down my nose in a coy gesture.

'Nick, you mustn't be jealous of other men. I have lots of men and I compete in a man's world. I am surrounded by them.'

She was referring to the graduate. She had missed my point. I was not jealous any more, I was just sad. Sad and tired and weary and old. This lust was hollow and worthless and so was Jordan.

'I have just made love to you,' I blurted.

Her lips parted and she looked faintly horrified.

'I said, I have just made—'

'I heard you.'

She turned away from me and began pulling on her clothes. Instead of watching her like I might have done, I began dressing too. We were silent and the room was oppressive.

'You've changed, Nick.'

'Yes.'

She didn't ask me why and I was glad.

I collected my jacket from downstairs and we stood awkwardly in the doorway.

'Goodbye.'

'See you soon,' I said, although we were both unsure.

Chapter Eighteen

After I left Jordan, I didn't know where to go. I walked down the road with a false, cheerful step, staring straight ahead and wondering what would happen next. For some inexplicable reason, my thoughts kept returning to Gatsby. I wanted to speak to him. I felt that he might understand my predicament. Jordan was no Daisy, but there were similarities.

I hailed a taxi and told him to stop off at a payphone. From there I called Gatsby's house, but the line was busy. I tried four times; finally an exasperated central told me the wire was being kept open for long distance from Detroit. Taking out my timetable, I drew a small circle around the three-fifty train. Then I told the taxi to drop me at the station and tried to think. It was just noon.

When I passed the ash heaps on the train that morning

I had crossed deliberately to the other side of the car. I supposed there'd be a curious crowd around there all day with little boys searching for dark spots in the dust, and some garrulous man telling over and over what had happened, until it became less and less real even to him and he could tell it no longer, and Myrtle Wilson's tragic achievement was forgotten. Now I want to go back a little and tell what happened at the garage after we left there the night before.

They had difficulty in locating the sister, Catherine. She must have broken her rule against drinking that night, for when she arrived she was stupid with liquor and unable to understand that the ambulance had already gone to Flushing. When they convinced her of this, she immediately fainted, as if that was the intolerable part of the affair. Someone, kind or curious, took her in his car and drove her in the wake of her sister's body. My sentiments are strange where Catherine is involved. I still think of her as a no-name person that I met at a party. I forget how intimate we were that night, I forget that night even. It seems like everything in my life – every woman in my life – has been eclipsed by Jordan Baker. Jordan Baker that hard, harsh winner.

Anyway, until long after midnight a changing crowd

lapped up against the front of the garage, while George Wilson rocked himself back and forth on the couch inside. For a while the door of the office was open, and everyone who came into the garage glanced irresistibly through it. Finally someone said it was a shame, and closed the door. Michaelis and several other men were with him; first, four or five men, later two or three men. Still later Michaelis had to ask the last stranger to wait there fifteen minutes longer, while he went back to his own place and made a pot of coffee. After that, he stayed there alone with Wilson until dawn.

About three o'clock the quality of Wilson's incoherent muttering changed – he grew quieter and began to talk about the yellow car. He announced that he had a way of finding out whom the yellow car belonged to, and then he blurted out that a couple of months ago his wife had come from the city with her face bruised and her nose swollen.

But when he heard himself say this, he flinched and began to cry 'Oh, my God!' again in his groaning voice. Michaelis made a clumsy attempt to distract him.

'How long have you been married, George? Come on there, try and sit still a minute and answer my question. How long have you been married?'

'Twelve years.'

'Ever had any children? Come on, George, sit still – I asked you a question. Did you ever have any children?'

The hard brown beetles kept thudding against the dull light, and whenever Michaelis heard a car go tearing along the road outside it sounded to him like the car that hadn't stopped a few hours before. He didn't like to go into the garage, because the workbench was stained where the body had been lying, so he moved uncomfortably around the office – he knew every object in it before morning – and from time to time sat down beside Wilson trying to keep him more quiet.

'Have you got a church you go to sometimes, George? Maybe even if you haven't been there for a long time? Maybe I could call up the church and get a priest to come over and he could talk to you, see?'

'Don't belong to any.'

'You ought to have a church, George, for times like this. You must have gone to church once. Didn't you get married in a church? Listen, George, listen to me. Didn't you get married in a church?'

'That was a long time ago.'

The effort of answering broke the rhythm of his rocking – for a moment he was silent. Then the same half-knowing, half-bewildered look came back into his faded eyes.

'Look in the drawer there,' he said, pointing at the desk.

'Which drawer?'

'That drawer – that one.'

Michaelis opened the drawer nearest his hand. There was nothing in it but a small, expensive dog-leash made of leather and braided silver. It was apparently new.

'This?' he enquired, holding it up.

Wilson stared and nodded.

'I found it yesterday afternoon. She tried to tell me about it, but I knew it was something funny.'

'You mean your wife bought it?'

'She had it wrapped in tissue paper on her bureau.'

Michaelis didn't see anything odd in that, and he gave Wilson a dozen reasons why his wife might have bought the dog-leash. But conceivably Wilson had heard some of these same explanations before, from Myrtle, because he began saying 'Oh, my God!' again in a whisper – his comforter left several explanations in the air.

'Then he killed her,' said Wilson. His mouth dropped open suddenly and his face grew both hard and pale.

'Who did?'

'I have a way of finding out.'

'You're morbid, George,' said his friend. 'This has been

275

a strain to you and you don't know what you're saying. You'd better try and sit quiet till morning.'

'He murdered her.'

'It was an accident, George.'

Wilson shook his head. His eyes narrowed and his mouth widened slightly with the ghost of a superior 'Hm!'

'I know,' he said definitely, 'I'm one of these trusting fellas and I don't think any harm to nobody, but when I get to know a thing I know it. It was the man in that car. She ran out to speak to him and he wouldn't stop.'

Michaelis had seen this too, but it hadn't occurred to him that there was any special significance in it. He believed that Mrs Wilson had been running away from her husband, rather than trying to stop any particular car.

'How could she of been like that?'

'She's a deep one,' said Wilson, as if that answered the question. 'Ah-h-h—'

He began to rock again, and Michaelis stood twisting the leash in his hand.

'Maybe you got some friend that I could telephone for, George?'

This was a forlorn hope – he was almost sure that Wilson had no friend: there was not enough of him for his wife. He was glad a little later when he noticed a change in the room, a blue quickening by the window, and realised that dawn wasn't far off. About five o'clock it was blue enough outside to snap off the light.

Wilson's glazed eyes turned out to the ash heaps, where small grey clouds took on fantastic shape and scurried here and there in the faint dawn wind.

'I spoke to her,' he muttered, after a long silence. 'I told her she might fool me but she couldn't fool God. I took her to the window,' – with an effort he got up and walked to the rear window and leaned with his face pressed against it – 'and I said "God knows what you've been doing, everything you've been doing. You may fool me, but you can't fool God!"'

Standing behind him, Michaelis saw with a shock that he was looking at the eyes of Dr T. J. Eckleburg, which had just emerged, pale and enormous, from the dissolving night.

'God sees everything,' repeated Wilson.

'That's an advertisement,' Michaelis assured him. Something made him turn away from the window and look back into the room. But Wilson stood there a long time, his face close to the window-pane, nodding into the twilight.

By six o'clock Michaelis was worn out, and grateful for

the sound of a car stopping outside. It was one of the watchers of the night before who had promised to come back, so he cooked breakfast for three, which he and the other man ate together. Wilson was quieter now, and Michaelis went home to sleep; when he awoke four hours later and hurried back to the garage, Wilson was gone.

His movements – he was on foot all the time – were afterwards traced to Port Roosevelt and then to Gad's Hill, where he bought a sandwich that he didn't eat, and a cup of coffee. He must have been tired and walking slowly, for he didn't reach Gad's Hill until noon. Thus far there was no difficulty in accounting for his time – there were boys who had seen a man 'acting sort of crazy', and motorists at whom he stared oddly from the side of the road. Then for three hours he disappeared from view. The police, on the strength of what he said to Michaelis, that he 'had a way of finding out', supposed that he spent that time going from garage to garage thereabout, enquiring for a yellow car. On the other hand, no garage man who had seen him ever came forward, and perhaps he had an easier, surer way of finding out what he wanted to know. By half-past two he was in West Egg, where he asked someone the way to Gatsby's house. So by that time he knew Gatsby's name.

At two o'clock Gatsby put on his bathing-suit and left word with the butler that if any one phoned word was to be brought to him at the pool. He stopped at the garage for a pneumatic mattress that had amused his guests during the summer, and the chauffeur helped him pump it up. Then he gave instructions that the open car wasn't to be taken out under any circumstances – and this was strange, because the front right fender needed repair.

Gatsby shouldered the mattress and started for the pool. Once he stopped and shifted it a little, and the chauffeur asked him if he needed help, but he shook his head and in a moment disappeared among the yellowing trees.

No telephone message arrived, but the butler went without his sleep and waited for it until four o'clock – until long after there was anyone to give it to if it came. I have an idea that Gatsby himself didn't believe it would come, and perhaps he no longer cared. If that was true he must have felt that he had lost the old warm world, paid a high price for living too long with a single dream. He must have looked up at an unfamiliar sky through frightening leaves and shivered as he found what a grotesque thing a rose is and how raw the sunlight was upon the scarcely created grass. A new world, material without being real, where poor ghosts, breathing dreams like air, drifted fortuitously about . . . like that ashen, fantastic figure gliding towards him through the amorphous trees.

The chauffeur – he was one of Wolfsheim's protégés – heard the shots – afterwards he could only say that he hadn't thought anything much about them. I drove from the station directly to Gatsby's house and my rushing anxiously up the front steps was the first thing that alarmed anyone. But they knew then, I firmly believe. With scarcely a word said, four of us, the chauffeur, butler, gardener, and I, hurried down to the pool.

There was a faint, barely perceptible movement of the water as the fresh flow from one end urged its way towards the drain at the other. With little ripples that were hardly the shadows of waves, the laden mattress moved irregularly down the pool. A small gust of wind that scarcely corrugated the surface was enough to disturb its accidental course with its accidental burden. The touch of a cluster of leaves revolved it slowly, tracing, like the leg of a compass, a thin red circle in the water.

It was after we started with Gatsby towards the house that the gardener saw Wilson's body a little way off in the grass, and the holocaust was complete.

Chapter Nineteen

After two years I remember the rest of that day, and that night and the next day, only as an endless drill of police and photographers and newspaper men in and out of Gatsby's front door. A rope stretched across the main gate and a policeman by it kept out the curious, but little boys soon discovered that they could enter through my yard, and there were always a few of them clustered open-mouthed about the pool. Someone with a positive manner, perhaps a detective, used the expression 'madman' as he bent over Wilson's body that afternoon, and the adventitious authority of his voice set the key for the newspaper reports next morning.

Most of those reports were a nightmare – grotesque, circumstantial, eager, and untrue. When Michaelis's testimony at the inquest brought to light Wilson's suspicions of his wife I thought the whole tale would shortly be served up in racy pasquinade – but Catherine, who might have said anything, didn't say a word. She showed a surprising amount of character about it too – looked at the coroner with determined eyes under that corrected brow of hers, and swore that her sister had never seen Gatsby, that her sister was completely happy with her husband, that her sister had been into no mischief whatever. She convinced herself of it, and cried into her handkerchief, as if the very suggestion was more than she could endure. S. Wilson was reduced to a man 'deranged by grief' in order that the case might remain in its simplest form. And it rested there.

But all this part of it seemed remote and unessential. I found myself on Gatsby's side, and alone. From the moment I telephoned news of the catastrophe to West Egg village, every surmise about him, and every practical question, was referred to me. At first I was surprised and confused; then, as he lay in his house and didn't move or breathe or speak, hour upon hour, it grew upon me that I was responsible, because no one else was interested – interested, I mean, with that intense personal interest to which everyone has some vague right at the end.

I called up Daisy half an hour after we found him, called

her instinctively and without hesitation. But she and Tom had gone away early that afternoon, and taken baggage with them.

'Left no address?'

'No.'

'Say when they'd be back?'

'No.'

'Any idea where they are? How I could reach them?'

'I don't know. Can't say.'

I wanted to get somebody for him. I wanted to go into the room where he lay and reassure him: 'I'll get somebody for you, Gatsby. Don't worry. Just trust me and I'll get somebody for you—'

Meyer Wolfsheim's name wasn't in the phone book. The butler gave me his office address on Broadway, and I called Information, but by the time I had the number it was long after five, and no one answered the phone.

'Will you ring again?'

'I've rung them three times.'

'It's very important.'

'Sorry. I'm afraid no one's there.'

I went back to the drawing room and thought for an instant that they were chance visitors, all these official people who suddenly filled it. But, as they drew back the sheet and looked at Gatsby with unmoved eyes, his protest continued in my brain:

'Look here, old sport, you've got to get somebody for me. You've got to try hard. I can't go through this alone.'

Someone started to ask me questions, but I broke away and going upstairs looked hastily through the unlocked parts of his desk – he'd never told me definitely that his parents were dead. But there was nothing – only the picture of Dan Cody, a token of forgotten violence, staring down from the wall.

Next morning I sent the butler to New York with a letter to Wolfsheim, which asked for information and urged him to come out on the next train. That request seemed superfluous when I wrote it. I was sure he'd start when he saw the newspapers, just as I was sure there'd be a wire from Daisy before noon – but neither a wire nor Mr Wolfsheim arrived; no one arrived except more police and photographers and newspaper men. When the butler brought back Wolfsheim's answer I began to have a feeling of defiance, of scornful solidarity between Gatsby and me against them all.

Dear Mr Carraway.
This has been one of the most terrible shocks of my life to me I hardly can believe it that it is true at all. Such

*a mad act as that man did should make us all think. I
cannot come down now as I am tied up in some very
important business and cannot get mixed up in this
thing now. If there is anything I can do a little later let
me know in a letter by Edgar. I hardly know where I
am when I hear about a thing like this and am
completely knocked down and out.*

    Yours truly
    Meyer Wolfsheim

and then hasty addenda beneath:

*Let me know about the funeral etc. do not know his
family at all.*

When the phone rang that afternoon and Long Distance
said Chicago was calling I thought this would be Daisy at
last. But the connection came through as a man's voice, very
thin and far away.

'This is Slagle speaking . . .'

'Yes?' The name was unfamiliar.

'Hell of a note, isn't it? Get my wire?'

'There haven't been any wires.'

'Young Parke's in trouble,' he said rapidly. 'They picked

him up when he handed the bonds over the counter. They got a circular from New York giving 'em the numbers just five minutes before. What d'you know about that, hey? You never can tell in these hick towns—'

'Hello!' I interrupted breathlessly. 'Look here – this isn't Mr Gatsby. Mr Gatsby's dead.'

There was a long silence on the other end of the wire, followed by an exclamation . . . then a quick squawk as the connection was broken.

I think it was on the third day that a telegram signed Henry C. Gatz arrived from a town in Minnesota. It said only that the sender was leaving immediately and to postpone the funeral until he came.

It was Gatsby's father, a solemn old man, very helpless and dismayed, bundled up in a long cheap ulster against the warm September day. His eyes leaked continuously with excitement, and when I took the bag and umbrella from his hands he began to pull so incessantly at his sparse grey beard that I had difficulty in getting off his coat. He was on the point of collapse, so I took him into the music room and made him sit down while I sent for something to eat. But he wouldn't eat, and the glass of milk spilled from his trembling hand.

'I saw it in the Chicago newspaper,' he said. 'It was all in the Chicago newspaper. I started right away.'

'I didn't know how to reach you.'

His eyes, seeing nothing, moved ceaselessly about the room.

'It was a madman,' he said. 'He must have been mad.'

'Wouldn't you like some coffee?' I urged him.

'I don't want anything. I'm all right now, Mr—'

'Carraway.'

'Well, I'm all right now. Where have they got Jimmy?' I took him into the drawing room, where his son lay, and left him there. Some little boys had come up on the steps and were looking into the hall; when I told them who had arrived, they went reluctantly away.

After a little while Mr Gatz opened the door and came out, his mouth ajar, his face flushed slightly, his eyes leaking isolated and unpunctual tears. He had reached an age where death no longer has the quality of ghastly surprise, and when he looked around him now for the first time and saw the height and splendour of the hall and the great rooms opening out from it into other rooms, his grief began to be mixed with an awed pride. I helped him to a bedroom upstairs; while he took off his coat and vest I told him that all arrangements had been deferred until he came.

'I didn't know what you'd want, Mr Gatsby—'

'Gatz is my name.'

'– Mr Gatz. I thought you might want to take the body West.'

He shook his head.

'Jimmy always liked it better down East. He rose up to his position in the East. Were you a friend of my boy's, Mr –?'

'We were close friends.'

'He had a big future before him, you know. He was only a young man, but he had a lot of brain power here.'

He touched his head impressively, and I nodded.

'If he'd of lived, he'd of been a great man. A man like James J. Hill. He'd of helped build up the country.'

'That's true,' I said, uncomfortably.

He fumbled at the embroidered coverlet, trying to take it from the bed, and lay down stiffly – was instantly asleep.

That night an obviously frightened person called up, and demanded to know who I was before he would give his name.

'This is Mr Carraway,' I said.

'Oh!' He sounded relieved. 'This is Klipspringer.'

I was relieved too, for that seemed to promise another friend at Gatsby's grave. I didn't want it to be in the papers and draw a sightseeing crowd, so I'd been calling up a few people myself. They were hard to find.

'The funeral's tomorrow,' I said. 'Three o'clock, here at the house. I wish you'd tell anybody who'd be interested.'

'Oh, I will,' he broke out hastily. 'Of course I'm not likely to see anybody, but if I do.'

His tone made me suspicious.

'Of course you'll be there yourself.'

'Well, I'll certainly try. What I called up about is—'

'Wait a minute,' I interrupted. 'How about saying you'll come?'

'Well, the fact is – the truth of the matter is that I'm staying with some people up here in Greenwich, and they rather expect me to be with them to-morrow. In fact, there's a sort of picnic or something. Of course I'll do my very best to get away.'

I ejaculated an unrestrained 'Huh!' and he must have heard me, for he went on nervously:

'What I called up about was a pair of shoes I left there. I wonder if it'd be too much trouble to have the butler send them on. You see, they're tennis shoes, and I'm sort of helpless without them. My address is care of B. F.—'

I didn't hear the rest of the name, because I hung up the receiver.

After that I felt a certain shame for Gatsby – one gentleman to whom I telephoned implied that he had got what he deserved. However, that was my fault, for he was one of those who used to sneer most bitterly at Gatsby on the courage of Gatsby's liquor, and I should have known better than to call him.

The morning of the funeral I went up to New York to see Meyer Wolfsheim; I couldn't seem to reach him any other way. The door that I pushed open, on the advice of an elevator boy, was marked *The Swastika Holding Company* and at first there didn't seem to be any one inside. But when I'd shouted 'hello' several times in vain, an argument broke out behind a partition, and presently a lovely Jewess appeared at an interior door and scrutinised me with black hostile eyes.

'Nobody's in,' she said. 'Mr Wolfsheim's gone to Chicago.'

The first part of this was obviously untrue, for someone had begun to whistle 'The Rosary' tunelessly, inside.

'Please say that Mr Carraway wants to see him.'

'I can't get him back from Chicago, can I?'

At this moment a voice, unmistakably Wolfsheim's, called 'Stella!' from the other side of the door.

'Leave your name on the desk,' she said quickly. 'I'll give it to him when he gets back.'

'But I know he's there.'

She took a step towards me and began to slide her hands indignantly up and down her hips.

'You young men think you can force your way in here any time,' she scolded. 'We're getting sick and tired of it. When I say he's in Chicago, he's in Chicago.'

I mentioned Gatsby.

'Oh – h!' She looked at me over again. 'Will you just – What was your name?'

She vanished. In a moment Meyer Wolfsheim stood solemnly in the doorway, holding out both hands. He drew me into his office, remarking in a reverent voice that it was a sad time for all of us, and offered me a cigar.

'My memory goes back to when I first met him,' he said. 'A young major just out of the army and covered over with medals he got in the war. He was so hard up he had to keep on wearing his uniform because he couldn't buy some regular clothes. First time I saw him was when he come into Winebrenner's poolroom at Forty-third Street and asked for a job. He hadn't eaten anything for a couple of days. "Come and have some lunch with me," I said. He ate more than four dollars' worth of food in half an hour.'

'Did you start him in business?' I enquired.

'Start him! I made him.'

'Oh.'

'I raised him up out of nothing, right out of the gutter. I saw right away he was a fine-appearing, gentlemanly young man, and when he told me he was at Oggsford I knew I could use him good. I got him to join up in the American Legion and he used to stand high there. Right off he did some work for a client of mine up to Albany. We were so thick like that in everything' – he held up two bulbous fingers – 'always together.'

I wondered if this partnership had included the World's Series transaction in 1919.

'Now he's dead,' I said after a moment. 'You were his closest friend, so I know you'll want to come to his funeral this afternoon.'

'I'd like to come.'

'Well, come then.'

The hair in his nostrils quivered slightly, and as he shook his head his eyes filled with tears.

'I can't do it – I can't get mixed up in it,' he said.

'There's nothing to get mixed up in. It's all over now.'

'When a man gets killed I never like to get mixed up in it in any way. I keep out. When I was a young man it was different – if a friend of mine died, no matter how, I stuck with them to the end. You may think that's sentimental, but I mean it – to the bitter end.'

I saw that for some reason of his own he was determined not to come, so I stood up.

'Are you a college man?' he enquired suddenly.

For a moment I thought he was going to suggest a 'gonnegtion' but he only nodded and shook my hand.

'Let us learn to show our friendship for a man when he is alive and not after he is dead,' he suggested. 'After that my own rule is to let everything alone.'

When I left his office the sky had turned dark and I got back to West Egg in a drizzle. After changing my clothes I went next door and found Mr Gatz walking up and down excitedly in the hall. His pride in his son and in his son's possessions was continually increasing and now he had something to show me.

'Jimmy sent me this picture.' He took out his wallet with trembling fingers. 'Look there.'

It was a photograph of the house, cracked in the corners and dirty with many hands. He pointed out every detail to me eagerly. 'Look there!' and then sought admiration from my eyes. He had shown it so often that I think it was more real to him now than the house itself.

'Jimmy sent it to me. I think it's a very pretty picture. It shows up well.'

'Very well. Had you seen him lately?'

'He come out to see me two years ago and bought me the house I live in now. Of course we was broke up when he run off from home, but I see now there was a reason for it. He knew he had a big future in front of him. And ever since he made a success he was very generous with me.' He seemed reluctant to put away the picture, held it for another minute, lingeringly, before my eyes. Then he returned the wallet and pulled from his pocket a ragged old copy of a book called *Hopalong Cassidy*.

'Look here, this is a book he had when he was a boy. It just shows you.'

He opened it at the back cover and turned it around for me to see. On the last flyleaf was printed the word Schedule, and the date, September 12, 1906, and underneath:

Rise from bed . . . .
6.00 a.m.
Dumbbell exercise and wall-scaling . . . . . .
6.15–6.30
Study electricity, etc . . . .
7.15–8.15
Work . . . .
8.30–4.30 p.m.
Baseball and sports . . . .

4.30–5.00
Practise elocution, poise and how to attain it
5.00–6.00
Study needed inventions . . . .
7.00–9.00
General Resolves No wasting time at Shafters or [a name, indecipherable] No more smokeing or chewing Bath every other day Read one improving book or magazine per week Save $5.00 {crossed out} $3.00 per week Be better to parents

'I come across this book by accident,' said the old man. 'It just shows you, don't it?'

'It just shows you.'

'Jimmy was bound to get ahead. He always had some resolves like this or something. Do you notice what he's got about improving his mind? He was always great for that. He told me I ate like a hog once, and I beat him for it.'

He was reluctant to close the book, reading each item aloud and then looking eagerly at me. I think he rather expected me to copy down the list for my own use.

A little before three the Lutheran minister arrived from Flushing, and I began to look involuntarily out the windows for other cars. So did Gatsby's father. And as the time passed and the servants came in and stood waiting in the hall, his eyes began to blink anxiously, and he spoke of the rain in a worried, uncertain way. The minister glanced several times at his watch, so I took him aside and asked him to wait for half an hour. But it wasn't any use. Nobody came.

About five o'clock our procession of three cars reached the cemetery and stopped in a thick drizzle beside the gate – first a motor hearse, horribly black and wet, then Mr Gatz and the minister and I in the limousine, and a little later four or five servants and the postman from West Egg in Gatsby's station wagon, all wet to the skin. As we started through the gate into the cemetery I heard a car stop and then the sound of someone splashing after us over the soggy ground. I looked around. It was the man with owl-eyed glasses whom I had found marvelling over Gatsby's books in the library one night three months before.

I'd never seen him since then. I don't know how he knew about the funeral, or even his name. The rain poured down his thick glasses, and he took them off and wiped them to see the protecting canvas unrolled from Gatsby's grave.

I tried to think about Gatsby then for a moment, but he was already too far away, and I could only remember, without resentment, that Daisy hadn't sent a message or a flower. Dimly I heard someone murmur, 'Blessed are the dead that the rain falls on,' and then the owl-eyed man said 'Amen to that,' in a brave voice.

We straggled down quickly through the rain to the cars. Owl-eyes spoke to me by the gate.

'I couldn't get to the house,' he remarked.

'Neither could anybody else.'

'Go on!' He started. 'Why, my God! They used to go there by the hundreds.' He took off his glasses and wiped them again, outside and in.

'The poor son of a bitch,' he said.

One of my most vivid memories is of coming back West from prep school and later from college at Christmas time. Those who went farther than Chicago would gather in the old dim Union Station at six o'clock of a December evening, with a few Chicago friends, already caught up into their own holiday gaieties, to bid them a hasty goodbye. I remember the fur coats of the girls returning from Miss This-or-that's and the chatter of frozen breath and the hands waving overhead as we caught sight of old acquaintances, and the matchings of invitations: 'Are you going to the Ordways'? the Herseys'? the Schultzes'?' and the long green tickets clasped tight in our gloved hands. And last the murky yellow cars of the Chicago, Milwaukee and St Paul railroad looking cheerful as Christmas itself on the tracks beside the gate.

When we pulled out into the winter night and the real snow, our snow, began to stretch out beside us and twinkle against the windows, and the dim lights of small Wisconsin stations moved by, a sharp wild brace came suddenly into the air. We drew in deep breaths of it as we walked back from dinner through the cold vestibules, unutterably aware of our identity with this country for one strange hour, before we melted indistinguishably into it again.

That's my Middle West – not the wheat or the prairies or the lost Swede towns, but the thrilling returning trains of my youth, and the street lamps and sleigh bells in the frosty dark and the shadows of holly wreaths thrown by lighted windows on the snow. I am part of that, a little solemn with the feel of those long winters, a little complacent from growing up in the Carraway house in a city where dwellings are still called through decades by a family's name. I see now that this has been a story of the West, after all – Tom and Gatsby, Daisy and Jordan and I, were all Westerners, and perhaps we possessed some deficiency in common which made us subtly unadaptable to Eastern life.

Even when the East excited me most, even when I was most keenly aware of its superiority to the bored, sprawling, swollen towns beyond the Ohio, with their interminable inquisitions which spared only the children and the very old – even then it had always for me a quality of distortion. West Egg, especially, still figures in my more fantastic dreams. I see it as a night scene by El Greco: a hundred houses, at once conventional and grotesque, crouching under a sullen, overhanging sky and a lustreless moon with shrieks of ecstasy and groans of pleasure echoing ominously in the distance. In the foreground four solemn men in dress suits are walking along the sidewalk with a stretcher on which lies a drunken woman in a white evening dress. Her hand, which dangles over the side, sparkles cold with jewels. Gravely the men turn in at a house – the wrong house. But no one knows the woman's name, and no one cares.

After Gatsby's death the East was haunted for me like that, distorted beyond my eyes' power of correction. So when the blue smoke of brittle leaves was in the air and the wind blew the wet laundry stiff on the line I decided to come back home.

There was one thing to be done before I left, an awkward, unpleasant thing that perhaps had better have been let alone. But I wanted to leave things in order and not just trust that obliging and indifferent sea to sweep my refuse away. I saw Jordan Baker and talked over and around what had happened to us together, and what had happened afterwards to me, and she lay perfectly still, listening, in a big chair at a club in town.

She was dressed to play golf, and I remember thinking she looked like a good illustration, her chin raised a little jauntily, her hair the colour of a smoking cigar, her face the same brown tint as the fingerless glove on her knee. For once I barely noticed her breasts or her lips or her legs. As seductive as she was, she was sexless to me. I had gorged myself to excess.

But her grey eyes still held some of their stirring power as they regarded me coolly throughout the meeting. A grey, solid shield. She was my first love, but she no longer drove me to obsession. She made me feel old and sad.

'You wanted something that I couldn't give to you,' her husky voice said suddenly.

I had just been talking about Gatsby so the comment took me by surprise.

'Everyone can love.'

'No they can't. Look at Daisy.'

She picked up one of her brown fingerless gloves and began putting it on, signalling that the conversation was over.

'I made love to you and you didn't like it,' I said.

I knew she didn't because instead of answering my question, she told me plainly that she was engaged to another man. I doubted that, though there were several she could have married at a nod of her head, but I pretended to be surprised. For just a minute I wondered if I wasn't making a mistake, then I thought it all over again quickly and got up to say goodbye.

'Nevertheless you've thrown me over,' said Jordan suddenly. 'I don't give a damn about you now, but it was a new experience for me, and I felt a little dizzy for a while.'

We shook hands.

I was grateful for that admittance. I was glad that I had managed to have some effect on her however small – glad that I had dented her grey shield just a fraction. At the time, it was enough for me, but then she ruined it.

'Oh, and do you remember,' – she added – 'a conversation we had once about driving a car?'

'Why – not exactly.'

'You said a bad driver was only safe until she met another bad driver? Well, I need another bad driver, don't I? I mean it was careless of me to make such a wrong guess. I thought you were rather a fun, wild person. I thought you would share in my secret.'

She smiled at me slyly, triumphantly.

'I'm thirty,' I said. 'I'm five years too old to lie to myself and call it honour.'

She didn't answer.

Angry, and still half in love with her, and tremendously sorry, I turned away.

One afternoon late in October I saw Tom Buchanan. He was walking ahead of me along Fifth Avenue in his alert, aggressive way, his hands out a little from his body as if to fight off interference, his head moving sharply here and there, adapting itself to his restless eyes. Just as I slowed up to avoid overtaking him he stopped and began frowning into the windows of a jewellery store. Suddenly he saw me and walked back, holding out his hand.

'What's the matter, Nick? Do you object to shaking hands with me?'

'Yes. You know what I think of you.'

'You're crazy, Nick,' he said quickly. 'Crazy as hell. I don't know what's the matter with you.'

'Tom,' I enquired, 'what did you say to Wilson that afternoon?'

He stared at me without a word, and I knew I had guessed right about those missing hours. I started to turn away, but he took a step after me and grabbed my arm.

'I told him the truth,' he said. 'He came to the door while we were getting ready to leave, and when I sent down word that we weren't in he tried to force his way upstairs. He was crazy enough to kill me if I hadn't told him who owned the car. His hand was on a revolver in his pocket every minute he was in the house—' He broke off defiantly. 'What if I did tell him? That fellow had it coming to him. He threw dust into your eyes just like he did in Daisy's, but he was a tough one. He ran over Myrtle like you'd run over a dog and never even stopped his car.'

There was nothing I could say, except the one unutterable fact that it wasn't true.

'And if you think I didn't have my share of suffering – look here, when I went to give up that flat and saw that damn box of dog biscuits sitting there on the sideboard, I sat down and cried like a baby. By God it was awful—'

I couldn't forgive him or like him, but I saw that what he had done was, to him, entirely justified. It was all very careless and confused. They were careless people, Tom and Daisy – they smashed up things and creatures and then retreated back into their money or their vast carelessness, or whatever it was that kept them together, and let other people clean up the mess they had made. That was Jordan too and that was why I couldn't have her.

I shook hands with him; it seemed silly not to, for I felt suddenly as though I were talking to a child. Then he went into the jewellery store to buy a pearl necklace – or perhaps only a pair of cuff buttons – rid of my provincial squeamishness for ever.

Gatsby's house was still empty when I left – the grass on his lawn had grown as long as mine. One of the taxi drivers in the village never took a fare past the entrance gate without stopping for a minute and pointing inside; perhaps it was he who drove Daisy and Gatsby over to East Egg the night of the accident, and perhaps he had made a story about it all his own. I didn't want to hear it and I avoided him when I got off the train.

I spent my Saturday nights in New York because those gleaming, dazzling parties of his were with me so vividly that I could still hear the music and the moans, faint and incessant, from his garden, and the cars going up and down his drive. One night I did hear a material car there, and saw its lights stop at his front steps. But I didn't investigate. Probably it was some final guest who had been away at the ends of the earth and didn't know that the party was over.

On the last night, with my trunk packed and my car sold to the grocer, I went over and looked at that huge incoherent failure of a house once more. On the white steps an obscene word, scrawled by some boy with a piece of brick, stood out clearly in the moonlight, and I erased it, drawing my shoe raspingly along the stone. Then I wandered down to the beach and sprawled out on the sand.

Most of the big shore places were closed now and there were hardly any lights except the shadowy, moving glow of a ferryboat across the Sound. And as the moon rose higher the inessential houses began to melt away until gradually I became aware of the old island here that flowered once for Dutch sailors' eyes – a fresh, green breast of the new world. Its vanished trees, the trees that had made way for Gatsby's house, had once pandered in whispers to the last and greatest of all human dreams; for a transitory enchanted moment man must have held his breath in the presence of this continent, compelled into an aesthetic contemplation he neither understood nor desired, face to face for the last time in history with something commensurate to his capacity for wonder.

And as I sat there brooding on the old, unknown world, I thought of Gatsby's wonder when he first picked out the green light at the end of Daisy's dock. He had come a long way to this blue lawn, and his dream must have seemed so close that he could hardly fail to grasp it. He did not know that it was already behind him, somewhere back in that vast obscurity beyond the city, where the dark fields of the republic rolled on under the night.

Gatsby believed in the green light, the orgastic future that year by year recedes before us. It eluded us then, but that's no matter – tomorrow we will run faster, stretch out our arms farther . . . And one fine morning –

So we beat on, boats against the current, borne back ceaselessly into the past.

Acknowledgements

Massive thank you to my amazing agent, Isabel Atherton from Creative Authors Ltd., who I would dance the Charleston with any night. A huge thanks also to everyone at Piatkus and Little, Brown, especially Donna Condon, Grace Menary-Winefield and Caroline Kirkpatrick – we can shimmy the Black Bottom. Thanks also to my family and friends, with particular mention of James. And very special appreciation to F. Scott Fitzgerald for being out of copyright.

FIFTY SHADES OF DORIAN GRAY

Oscar Wilde and
Nicole Audrey Spector

Night after night she awoke in a feverish sweat, her hips writhing on their own accord, the bed sheet balled in a coil and clenched between her legs. It was so . . . real. Like he'd really been there.

First published to sensational scandal amidst accusations that the novel was hedonist, unclean and depicted distorted views of morality, *The Picture of Dorian Gray* was a hit back in the day. In 1890, the *Daily Chronicle* wrote that Wilde's novel 'will taint every young mind that comes in contact with it.' Well, Victorian critics, gird your loins and prepare to meet Nicole Audrey Spector's *Fifty Shades of Dorian Gray*: hotter, lewder, sexier, steamier and more morally corrupt than Oscar Wilde's original story!

Rediscover this celebrated novel as it traces the moral degeneration of a beautiful young Londoner seduced by art and beauty into a cruel and reckless pursuer of pleasure. Meet artist Rosemary Hall and follow her inevitable downfall brought by her lust for the famous Dorian Gray . With a mix of old-fashioned Victorian debauchery and erotic 21st-century lust, this cleverly sexed-up classic will leave you wanting more!

It's a tale both familiar and new in this brilliant erotic mash-up of one of Oscar Wilde's most talked-about and cautionary tales: *Fifty Shades of Grey* meets *The Picture of Dorian Gray*.

JANE EYROTICA

Charlotte Brontë and
Karena Rose

*Holding my gaze, he removed a curtain tie from one of the
bedsteads. I was confused when he uttered huskily,
'Put your hands out in front of you.' I obeyed.*

Jane Eyre has lived a sheltered life. Orphaned at a young age,
she is shipped off to Lowood School and can only dream of
tenderness and affection. Upon accepting a governess position at
Thornfield Hall, a world of passion, desire and sex explodes
before her naive eyes in the form of the brooding,
dashing master of the house: Mr Rochester.

After playful attempts to evade Mr Rochester's advances,
Jane finds herself succumbing to his savage, brutal lust and losing
herself in the intense heat of her yearning. Jane believes that
beneath Mr Rochester's dark, handsome, and sometimes brutal
exterior there must be a heart, and she is desperate to find love in
his hungry caresses. But then, she discovers something in the
attic . . . and her world is turned upside down for ever.

Sex collides with corsets in a burst of erotic ecstasy and
dark secrets, and one of literature's finest novels will
never be read the same again.